Frank Richard Stockton, Margaret Armstrong

A story-teller's pack

Frank Richard Stockton, Margaret Armstrong

A story-teller's pack

ISBN/EAN: 9783743367180

Manufactured in Europe, USA, Canada, Australia, Japa

Cover: Foto ©Andreas Hilbeck / pixelio.de

Manufactured and distributed by brebook publishing software (www.brebook.com)

Frank Richard Stockton, Margaret Armstrong

A story-teller's pack

WE WERE CARRYING MISS BURROUGHS TO THE BARN.

A Story-teller's Pack. By
Frank R. Stockton

Illustrated by Peter Newell, W. T. Smedley
Frank O. Small, Alice Barber Stephens, and
E. W. Kemble : : : : : : : : : : : : : : : :

Charles Scribner's Sons
New York ~~~~~ 1897

CONTENTS

LIST OF ILLUSTRATIONS

A FEW WORDS TO BEGIN WITH

A FEW WORDS TO BEGIN WITH

THE Story-teller puts down his pack, not a very heavy one, and if any of those who gather around him desire to know anything about the tales he bears, which shall be a little more interesting than a mere recital of their names in order, he will most gladly say a few words about them.

Here, now, is "The Magic Egg," and it is not everyone who, upon reading this story will believe that all of the things told therein could have happened. Of course, there are those who never, under any circumstances, believe anything magical, but then, there are other persons who will believe in magic, provided it shall appear reasonable. Now, if the happenings in this story seem unreasonable to anyone, let him or her wait until the middle of the first decade of the twentieth century. By that time, no doubt, the story will be easier to believe.

As to "The Staying Power of Sir Rohan," it may be remarked that the story controverts a very popular belief among horsemen, to the effect that a roan horse has never anything the matter with him. Now, there can be nothing more to the detriment of a horse than for him to know too much. What loves have been affected, what fortunes have been swayed, what ambitions have been aided and thwarted by over-knowledge in horses—or men!

This being the age of womanly endeavor, it was pleasant to chronicle, in "The Widow's Cruise," the very successful endeavor of a good woman, not only to rise to the level of the male maritime yarn, but to soar above it, and to look with pardonable contempt upon certain persons of the contrary sex, who had under-estimated her mental grasp.

For "Love Before Breakfast," the Story-teller has a certain affectionate feeling, because the scene of the story and all its surroundings are those of his own home. The characters mentioned never came upon that scene, nor did any of the incidents happen there ; but it is always most interesting, both to writer and reader, when unreal personages can be made to inhabit perfectly real places.

"The Bishop's Ghost and the Printer's Baby" was suggested by the tomb of Chaucer, in Westminster Abbey. The Story-teller was standing by that ancient sepulchre, when he perceived that some of the mortar under the stone lid had crumbled, and had fallen out, and naturally came the thought that out of such a little crack might gently slip the ghost of the poet, like a faint mist from "that pure well of English undefiled," floating quietly, here and there, among the old effigies and inscriptions, and touching now and then some noble visage, or some honored name with moist regard.

Had it not been for the enchanting scent of balmy salt water which hangs in the summer air along the southern coast of Cape Cod, "Captain Eli" would not have been the man he was, and of course, in that case, one of his ears would not have been better than the other. The world is full of good-hearted and noble sailors, but it is in the atmosphere of Nantucket Island and Buzzard's Bay that the "Old Captain" gently ripens into his most perfect fruition. If "Captain Eli" and "Cap-

tain Cephas" are not quite ripe, there is hope
for them.   They are living yet.

It was on a beautiful day in summer that
the Story-teller lay in a hammock and looked
up between the branches of a wide-spreading
tree, into the clear blue sky, and while gazing
into that mystical region of incomprehensible
space, he began to wonder what he would
think if suddenly he saw, in the midst of all
that delicate blue, a little black speck. What
could such a speck be? Where could it come
from? Presently that speck did appear. It
was the idea of the story, "As One Woman
to Another."

It may be that to many persons who own a
country home, the story of "My Well, and
What Came Out of It" may possess a pe-
culiar interest—perhaps a pleasant interest,
perhaps otherwise ; and if such persons
should at any time put themselves into the
hands of a man with a divining twig, they will
have good reason to expect to get a great deal
more than water. The opinions, the advice,
the remonstrances, the encouragements, the
pessimism, and the optimism which will well
up from the souls of their contiguous fellow-
beings will surprise them more, it may be

than if a stream of the purest Apollinaris
had spouted high into the air.

"Stephen Skarridge's Christmas" was written long ago, and was intended for the holiday number of *Punchinello*, that comic journal which flourished in New York before
Puck dropped one end of his girdle upon
Manhattan Island, or *Life* began. But the
merry journal died before the story was
printed, and "Mr. Skarridge" appeared in
the old *Scribner's Monthly*. Those were the
days of the old-fashioned Christmas story,
and, under the inspiration of those delightful "Carols" and "Chimes" which revived
among us the love of the Yule-tide, there
sprang up in this country, as well as in Eng-
land, a flourishing crop of Christmas stories,
all fashioned and shaped, as nearly as their
authors could make them, like unto their
shining prototypes. As so many people were
writing Christmas stories, this Story-teller
thought that he would try his hand.

Many a marriage in story and in real life
has depended upon the joining of estates;
but in the old-fashioned stories it was almost
always the case that if the estates did not
adjoin at the beginning of the story, they did

not do so at the end.   It was otherwise with
" My Unwilling Neighbor."   When Fate en-
ters into the service of love, it may not be
able, like Faith, to move mountains, but it
can do good work.

The Story-teller has nothing more to tell
about the contents of his Pack ; it is now the
turn of the buyer to have his say.

THE MAGIC EGG

THE MAGIC EGG

THE pretty little theatre attached to the building of the Unicorn Club had been hired for a certain January afternoon by Mr. Herbert Loring, who wished to give therein a somewhat novel performance to which he had invited a small audience consisting entirely of friends and acquaintances.

Loring was a handsome fellow about thirty years old, who had travelled far and studied much. He had recently made a long sojourn in the far East, and his friends had been invited to the theatre to see some of the wonderful things he had brought from that country of wonders. As Loring was a clubman, and belonged to a family of good social standing, his circle of acquaintances was large, and in this circle a good many unpleasant remarks had been made regarding the proposed entertainment—made, of course, by the people who had not been invited to be present. Some of the gossip on the subject had reached Loring, who did not hesitate to say that he could not talk to a crowd, and that he did not care to show the curious things he had collected to people who would not thoroughly appreciate them. He had been very particular in regard to his invitations.

At three o'clock on the appointed afternoon nearly all the people who had been invited to the Unicorn theatre were in their seats. No one had stayed away except for some very good reason, for it was well known that if Herbert Loring offered to show anything it was worth seeing.

About forty people were present, who sat talking to one another, or admiring the decoration of the theatre. As Loring stood upon the stage—where he was entirely alone, his exhibition requiring no assistants—he gazed through a loophole in the curtain upon a very interesting array of faces. There were the faces of many men and women of society, of students, of workers in various fields of thought, and even of idlers in all fields of thought, but there was not one which indicated a frivolous or listless disposition. The owners of those faces had come to see something, and they wished to see it.

For a quarter of an hour after the time announced for the opening of the exhibition Loring peered through the hole in the curtain, and then, although all the people he had expected had not arrived, he felt it would not do for him to wait any longer. The audience was composed of well-bred and courteous men and women, but despite their polite self-restraint Loring could see that some of them were getting tired of waiting. So, very reluctantly, and feeling that further delay was impossible, he raised the curtain and came forward on the stage.

Briefly he announced that the exhibition would open with some fireworks he had brought from Corea. It was plain to see that the statement that fireworks were about to be set off on a theatre stage, by an amateur, had rather startled some of the audience, and Loring hastened to explain that these were not real fireworks, but that they were contrivances made of colored glass, which were illuminated by the powerful lens of a lantern which was placed out of sight, and while the apparent pyrotechnic display would resemble fireworks of strange and grotesque designs, it would be absolutely without danger. He brought out some little bunches of bits of colored glass, hung them at some distance apart on a wire which was stretched across the stage just high enough for him to reach it, and then lighted his lantern, which he placed in one of the wings, lowered all the lights in the theatre, and began his exhibition.

As Loring turned his lantern on one of the clusters of glass lenses, strips, and points, and, unseen himself, caused them to move by means of long cords attached, the effects were beautiful and marvellous. Little wheels of colored fire rapidly revolved, miniature rockets appeared to rise a few feet and to explode in the air, and while all the ordinary forms of fireworks were produced on a diminutive scale, there were some effects that were entirely novel to the audience. As the light was turned successively upon one and another of the clusters of glass, sometimes it would flash along the whole line so rapidly that all the various combinations of color and motion seemed to be combined in one, and then for a time each particular set of fireworks would blaze, sparkle, and coruscate by itself, scattering particles of colored light, as if they had been real sparks of fire.

This curious and beautiful exhibition of miniature pyrotechnics was extremely interesting to the audience, who gazed upward with rapt and eager attention at the line of wheels, stars, and revolving spheres. So far as interest gave evidence of satisfaction, there was never a better satisfied audience. At first there had been some hushed murmurs of pleasure, but very soon the attention of every one seemed so completely engrossed by the dazzling display that they simply gazed in silence.

For twenty minutes or longer the glittering show went on, and not a sign of weariness or inattention was made by any one of the assembled company. Then gradually the colors of the little fireworks faded, the stars and wheels revolved more slowly, the lights in the body of the theatre were gradually raised, and the stage curtain went softly down.

Anxiously, and a little pale, Herbert Loring peered through the loophole in the curtain. It was not easy to judge of the effects of his exhibition, and he did not know whether or not it had been a success. There was no applause, but, on the other hand, there was no signs that any one resented the exhibition as a childish display of colored lights. It was impossible to look upon that audience without believing that they had been thoroughly interested in what they had seen, and that they expected to see more.

For two or three minutes Loring gazed through his loophole and then, still with some doubt in his heart, but with a little more color in his cheeks, he prepared for the second part of his performance.

At this moment there entered the theatre, at the very back of the house, a young lady. She was handsome and well-dressed, and as she opened the door—Loring had employed no ushers or other assistants in this little social performance—she paused for a moment and looked into the theatre, and then noiselessly stepped to a chair in the back row, and sat down.

This was Edith Starr, who, a month before, had been betrothed to Herbert Loring. Edith and her mother had been invited to this performance, and front seats had been reserved for them, for each guest had received a numbered card ; but Mrs. Starr had a head-ache, and could not go out that afternoon, and for a time her daughter had thought that she too must give up the pleasure Loring had promised her, and stay with her mother. But when the elder lady dropped into a quiet sleep, Edith thought that, late as it was, she would go by herself, and see what she could of the performance.

She was quite certain that if her presence were known to Loring he would stop what-ever he was doing until she had been pro-vided with a seat which he thought suitable for her, for he had made a point of her being properly seated when he gave the invitations. Therefore, being equally desirous of not dis-turbing the performance and of not being her-self conspicuous, she sat behind two rather large men, where she could see the stage per-fectly well, but where she herself would not be likely to be seen.

In a few moments the curtain rose, and Lor-ing came forward, carrying a small, light table, which he placed near the front of the stage, and for a moment stood quietly by it. Edith noticed upon his face the expression of uncertainty and anxiety which had not yet left it. Standing by the side of the table, and speaking very slowly, but so clearly that his words could be heard distinctly in all parts of the room, he began some introductory remarks regarding the second part of his performance.

"The extraordinary, and I may say marvellous, thing which I am about to show you," he said, "is known among East Indian magicians as the magic egg. The exhibition is a very uncommon one, and has seldom been seen by Americans or Europeans, and it was by a piece of rare good fortune that I became possessed of the appliances necessary for this exhibition. They are indeed very few and simple, but never before, to the best of my knowledge and belief, have they been seen outside of India.

"I will now get the little box which contains the articles necessary for this magical performance, and I will say that if I had time to tell you of the strange and amazing adventure which resulted in my possession of this box, I am sure you would be as much interested in that as I expect you to be in the contents of the box. But, in order that none of you may think this is an ordinary trick, executed by means of concealed traps or doors, I wish you to take particular notice of this table, which is, as you see, a plain, unpainted pine table with nothing but a flat top, and four straight legs at the corners. You can see under and around it, and it gives no opportunity to conceal anything." Then standing for a few moments as if he had something else to say, he turned and stepped toward one of the wings.

Edith was troubled as she looked at her lover during these remarks. Her interest was great; greater, indeed, than that of the people about her; but it was not a pleasant interest. As Loring stopped speaking, and looked about him, there was a momentary flush on his face. She knew this was caused by excitement, and she was pale from the same cause.

Very soon Loring came forward, and stood by the table.

"Here is the box," he said, "of which I spoke, and as I hold it up I think you can all see it. It is not large, being certainly not more than twelve inches in length and two deep, but it contains some very wonderful things. The outside of this box is covered with delicate engraving and carving which you cannot see, and these marks and lines have, I think, some magical meaning, but I do not know what it is. I will now open the box, and show you what is inside. The first thing I take out is this little stick, not thicker than a lead-pencil, but somewhat longer, as you see. This is a magical wand, and is covered with inscriptions of the same character as those on the outside of the box. The next thing is this little red bag, well-filled, as you see, which I shall put on the table, for I shall not yet need it.

"Now I take out a piece of cloth which is folded into a very small compass, but as I unfold it you will perceive that it is more than a foot square, and is covered with embroidery. All those strange lines and figures in gold and red, which you can plainly see on the cloth as I hold it up, are also characters in the same magic language as those on the box and wand. I will now spread the cloth on the table, and then take out the only remaining thing in the box, and this is nothing in the world but an egg—a simple, ordinary hen's egg, as you all see as I hold it up. It may be a trifle larger than an ordinary egg, but then, after all, it is nothing but a common egg—that is, in appearance; in reality it is a good deal more.

"Now I will begin the performance," and as he stood by the back of the table over which he had been slightly bending, and threw his eyes over the audience, his voice was stronger, and his face had lost all its pallor. He was evidently warming up with his subject.

"I now take up this wand," he said, "which, while I hold it, gives me power to produce the phenomena which you are about to behold. You may not all believe that there is any magic whatever about this little performance, and that it is all a bit of machinery; but whatever you may think about it, you shall see what you shall see.

"Now with this wand I gently touch this egg which is lying on the square of cloth. I do not believe you can see what has happened to this egg, but I will tell you. There is a little line, like a hair, entirely around it. Now that line has become a crack. Now you can see it, I know. It grows wider and wider! Look! The shell of the egg is separating in the middle. The whole egg slightly moves. Do you notice that? Now you can see something yellow showing itself between the two parts of the shell. See! It is moving a good deal, and the two halves of the shell are separating more and more! And now out tumbles this queer little object. Do you see what it is? It is a poor, weak, little chick, not able to stand, but alive—alive! You can all perceive that it is alive. Now you can see that it is standing on its feet, feebly enough, but still standing.

"Behold, it takes a few steps! You cannot doubt that it is alive, and came out of that egg. It is beginning to walk about over the cloth. Do you notice that it is picking the embroidery? Now, little chick, I will give you something to eat. This little red bag contains grain, a magical grain, with which I shall feed the chicken. You must excuse my awkwardness in opening the bag, as I still hold the wand; but this little stick I must not drop. See, little chick, there are some grains. They look like rice, but, in fact, I have no idea what they are. But he knows, he knows! Look at him! See how he picks it up! There! He has swallowed one, two, three. That will do, little chick, for a first meal.

"The grain seems to have strengthened him already, for see how lively he is, and how his yellow down stands out on him, so puffy and warm! You are looking for some more grain, are you? Well, you cannot have it just yet, and keep away from those pieces of egg-shell, which, by the way, I will put back into the box. Now, sir, try to avoid the edge of the table, and, to quiet you, I will give you a little tap on the back with my wand. Now, then, please observe closely. The down which just now covered him has almost gone. He is really a good deal bigger, and ever so much uglier. See the little pin - feathers sticking out over him! Some spots, here and there are almost bare, but he is ever so much more active. Ha! Listen to that! He is so strong that you can hear his beak as he pecks at the table. He is actually growing bigger and bigger before our very eyes! See that funny little tail, how it begins to stick up, and quills are showing at the end of his wings.

"Another tap, and a few more grains. Careful, sir! Don't tear the cloth! See how rapidly he grows! He is fairly covered with feathers, red and black, with a tip of yellow in front. You could hardly get that fellow into an ostrich egg! Now, then, what do you think of him? He is big enough for a broiler, though I don't think anyone would want to take him for that purpose. Some more grain, and another tap from my wand. See! He does not mind the little stick, for he has been used to it from his very birth. Now, then, he is what you would call a good half-grown chick. Rather more than half grown, I should say. Do you notice his tail? There is no mistaking him for a pullet. The long feathers are beginning to curl over, already. He must have a little more grain. Look out, sir or you will be off the table! Come back here! This table is too small for him, but if he were on the floor you could not see him so well.

"Another tap. Now see that comb on the top of his head; you scarcely noticed it before, and now it is bright red. And see his spurs beginning to show—on good thick legs, too. There is a fine young fellow for you! Look how he jerks his head from side to side, like the young prince of a poultry-yard, as he well deserves to be!"

The attentive interest which had at first characterized the audience now changed to excited admiration and amazement. Some leaned forward with mouths wide open. Others stood up so that they could see better. Ejaculations of astonishment and wonder were heard on every side, and a more thoroughly fascinated and absorbed audience was never seen.

"Now, my friends," Loring continued, "I will give this handsome fowl another tap. Behold the result—a noble, full-grown cock! Behold his spurs; they are nearly an inch long! See, there is a comb for you; and what a magnificent tail of green and black, contrasting so finely with the deep red of the rest of his body! Well, sir, you are truly too big for this table. As I cannot give you more room, I will set you up higher. Move over a little, and I will set this chair on the table. There! Up on the seat! That's right, but don't stop; there is the back, which is higher yet! Up with you! Ha! There, he nearly upset the chair, but I will hold it. See! He has turned around. Now, then, look at him. See his wings as he flaps them! He could fly with such wings. Look at him! See that swelling breast! Ha, Ha! Listen! Did you ever hear a crow like that? It fairly rings through the house. Yes; I knew it! There is another!"

At this point, the people in the house were in a state of wild excitement. Nearly all of them were on their feet, and they were in such a condition of frantic enthusiasm that Loring was afraid some of them might make a run for the stage.

"Come, sir," cried Loring, now almost shouting, "that will do; you have shown us the strength of your lungs. Jump down on the seat of the chair, now on the table. There, I will take away the chair, and you can stand for a moment on the table, and let our friends look at you, but only for a moment. Take that tap on your back. Now do you see any difference? Perhaps you may not, but I do. Yes; I believe you all do. He is not the big fellow he was a minute ago. He is really smaller; only a fine cockerel. A nice tail that, but with none of the noble sweep that it had a minute ago. No; don't try to get off the table. You can't escape my wand. Another tap. Behold a half-grown chicken, good to eat, but with not a crow in him. Hungry, are you? But you need not pick at the table that way. You get no more grain, but only this little tap. Ha! Ha! What are you coming to? There is a chicken barely feathered enough for us to tell what color he is going to be.

"Another tap will take still more of the conceit out of him. Look at him! There are his pin-feathers, and his bare spots. Don't try to get away; I can easily tap you again. Now, then. Here is a lovely little chick, fluffy with yellow down. He is active enough, but I shall quiet him. One tap, and now what do you see? A poor feeble chicken, scarcely able to stand, with his down all packed close to him as if he had been out in the rain. Ah, little chick, I will take the two halves of the egg-shell from which you came, and put them on each side of you. Come now, get in! I close them up; you are lost to view. There is nothing to be seen but a crack around the shell! Now it has gone! There, my friends, as I hold it on high, behold the magic egg, exactly as it was when I first took it out of the box, into which I will place it again, with the cloth and the wand and the little red bag, and shut it up with a snap. I will let you take one more look at this box before I put it away behind the scenes. Are you satisfied with what I have shown you? Do you think it is really as wonderful as you supposed it would be? "

At these words the whole audience burst into riotous applause, during which Loring disappeared; but he was back in a moment.

"Thank you!" he cried, bowing low, and waving his arms before him in the manner of an Eastern magician making a salaam. From side to side he turned, bowing and thanking, and then with a hearty, "Good-by to you, good-by to you all!" he stepped back, and let down the curtain.

For some moments the audience remained in their seats as if they were expecting something more, and then they rose quietly and began to disperse. Most of them were acquainted with one another, and there was a good deal of greeting and talking as they went out of the theatre.

When Loring was sure the last person had departed, he turned down the lights, locked the door, and gave the key to the steward of the club.

He walked to his home a happy man. His

exhibition had been a perfect success, with not a break or a flaw in it from beginning to end.

"I feel," thought the young man, as he strode along, "as if I could fly to the top of that steeple, and flap and crow until all the world heard me."

That evening, as was his daily custom, Herbert Loring called upon Miss Starr. He found the young lady in the library.

"I came in here," she said, "because I have a good deal to talk to you about, and I do not want interruptions."

With this arrangement the young man expressed his entire satisfaction, and immediately began to inquire the cause of her absence from his exhibition in the afternoon.

"But I was there," said Edith. "You did not see me, but I was there. Mother had a headache, and I went by myself."

"You were there!" exclaimed Loring, almost starting from his chair. "I don't understand. You were not in your seat."

"No," answered Edith; "I was on the very back row of seats. You could not see me, and I did not wish you to see me."

"Edith!" exclaimed Loring, rising to his

feet, and leaning over the library table, which was between them. "When did you come? How much of the performance did you see?"

"I was late," she said; "I did not arrive until after the fireworks, or whatever they were."

For a moment Loring was silent, as if he did not understand the situation.

"Fireworks!" he said. "How did you know there had been fireworks?"

"I heard the people talking of them as they left the theatre," she answered.

"And what did they say?" he inquired, quickly.

"They seemed to like them very well," she replied, "but I do not think they were quite satisfied. From what I heard some persons say, I inferred that they thought it was not very much of a show to which you had invited them."

Again Loring stood in thought, looking down at the table; but before he could speak again, Edith sprang to her feet.

"Herbert Loring," she cried, "what does all this mean? I was there during the whole of the exhibition of what you called the magic egg. I saw all those people wild with excitement at the wonderful sight of the chicken that came out of the egg, and grew to full size, and then dwindled down again, and went back into the egg, and, Herbert, there was no egg, and there was no little box, and there was no wand, and no embroidered cloth, and there was no red bag, nor any little chick, and there was no full-grown fowl, and there was no chair that you put on the table! There was nothing, absolutely nothing, but you and that table! And even the table was not what you said it was. It was not an unpainted pine table with four straight legs. It was a table of dark polished wood, and it stood on a single post with feet. There was nothing there that you said was there; everything was a sham and a delusion; every word you spoke was untrue. And yet everybody in that theatre, excepting you and me, saw all the things that you said were on the stage. I know they saw them all, for I was with the people, and heard them, and saw them, and at times I fairly felt the thrill of enthusiasm which possessed them as they glared at the miracles and wonders you said were happening."

Loring smiled. "Sit down, my dear Edith,"

he said. "You are excited, and there is not the slightest cause for it. I will explain the whole affair to you. It is simple enough. You know that study is the great object of my life. I study all sorts of things, and just now I am greatly interested in hypnotism. The subject has become fascinating to me; I have made a great many successful trials of my power, and the affair of this afternoon was nothing but a trial of my powers on a more extensive scale than anything I have yet attempted. I wanted to see if it were possible for me to hypnotize a considerable number of people without anyone suspecting what I intended to do. The result was a success. I hypnotized all those people by means of the first part of my performance, which consisted of some combinations of colored glass with lights thrown upon them. They revolved, and looked like fireworks, and were strung on a wire high up on the stage.

"I kept up the glittering and dazzling show —which was well worth seeing, I can assure you—until the people had been straining their eyes upward for almost half an hour; and this sort of thing—I will tell you if you

do not know it—is one of the methods of
producing hypnotic sleep.

"There was no one present who was not
an impressionable subject, for I was very
careful in sending out my invitations, and
when I became almost certain that my audience was thoroughly hypnotized, I stopped
the show, and began the real exhibition,
which was not really for their benefit, but for
mine.

"Of course, I was dreadfully anxious for
fear I had not succeeded entirely, and that
there might be at least some-one person who
had not succumbed to the hypnotic influences,
and so I tested the matter by bringing out
that table, and telling them it was something
it was not. If I had had any reason for supposing that some of the audience saw the
table as it really was, I had an explanation
ready, and I could have retired from my position without any one supposing that I had
intended making hypnotic experiments. The
rest of the exhibition would have been some
things that any one could see, and as soon as
possible I would have released from their
spell those who were hypnotized. But when
I became positively assured that every one

saw a light pine table with four straight legs, I confidently went on with the performances of the magic egg."

Edith Starr was still standing by the library table. She had not heeded Loring's advice to sit down, and she was trembling with emotion.

"Herbert Loring," she said, "you invited my mother and me to that exhibition. You gave us tickets for front seats, where we would be certain to be hypnotized if your experiment succeeded, and you would have made us see that false show, which faded from those people's minds as soon as they recovered from the spell ; for as they went away they were talking only of the fireworks, and not one of them mentioned a magic egg, or a chicken, or anything of the kind. Answer me this : did you not intend that I should come and be put under that spell ?"

Loring smiled. "Yes," he said, "of course I did; but then your case would have been different from that of the other spectators, I should have explained the whole thing to you, and I am sure we would have had a great deal of pleasure, and profit too, in discussing your experiences. The subject is extremely——"

"Explain to me!" she cried. "You would not have dared to do it! I do not know how brave you may be, but I know you would not have had the courage to come here and tell me that you had taken away my reason and my judgment, as you took them away from all those people, and that you had made me a mere tool of your will—glaring and panting with excitement at the wonderful things you told me to see where nothing existed. I have nothing to say about the others; they can speak for themselves if they ever come to know what you did to them. I speak for myself. I stood up with the rest of the people. I gazed with all my power, and over and over again I asked myself if it could be possible that anything was the matter with my eyes or my brain, and if I could be the only person there who could not see the marvellous spectacle that you were describing. But now I know that nothing was real, not even the little pine table, not even the man!"

"Not even me!" exclaimed Loring. "Surely I was real enough!"

"On that stage, yes," she said; "but you there proved you were not the Herbert Loring to whom I promised myself. He was an

unreal being. If he had existed he would
not have been a man who would have brought
me to that public place, all ignorant of his
intentions, to cloud my perceptions, to subject my intellect to his own, and make me
believe a lie. If a man should treat me in
that way once he would treat me so at other
times, and in other ways, if he had the chance.
You have treated me in the past as to-day you
treated those people who glared at the magic
egg. In the days gone by you made me see
an unreal man, but you will never do it again!
Good-by."

"Edith," cried Loring, "you don't——"

But she had disappeared through a side-
door, and he never spoke to her again.

Walking home through the dimly lighted
streets, Loring involuntarily spoke aloud:

"And this," he said, "is what came out of
the magic egg!"

THE STAYING POWER OF SIR ROHAN

THE STAYING POWER OF SIR ROHAN

DURING the winter in which I reached my twenty-fifth year, I lived with my mother's brother, Dr. Alfred Morris, in War-burton, a small country town, and I was there beginning the practice of medicine. I had been graduated in the spring, and my uncle earnestly advised me to come to him and act as his assistant, which advice, considering the fact that he was an elderly man, and that I might hope to succeed him in his excellent practice, was considered good advice by myself and my family.

At this time I practised very little, but learned a great deal, for as I often accompanied my uncle on his professional visits, I could not have taken a better post-graduate course. I had an invitation to spend the Christmas of that year with the Colling-woods, who had opened their country house, about twelve miles from Warburton, for the entertainment of a holiday house party. I had gladly accepted the invitation, and on the day before Christmas I went to the livery stable in the village to hire a horse and sleigh for the trip. At the stable I met "Uncle Beamish," who had also come to hire a conveyance.

Uncle Beamish, as he was generally called in the village, although I am sure he had no nephews or nieces in the place, was an elderly man who had retired from some business, I know not what, and was apparently quite able to live upon whatever income he had. He was a good man, rather illiterate, but very shrewd. Generous in good works, I do not think he was fond of giving away money, but his services were at the call of all who needed them.

I liked Uncle Beamish very much, for he was not only a good story-teller, but he was willing to listen to my stories, and when I found he wanted to hire a horse and sleigh to go to the house of his married sister, with whom he intended to spend Christmas, and that his sister lived on Upper Hill turnpike, on which road the Collingwood house was situated, I proposed that we should hire a sleigh together.

"That will suit me," said Uncle Beamish. "There couldn't have been a better fit if I had been measured for it. Less than half a mile after you turn into the turnpike, you pass my sister's house; then you can drop me and go on to the Collingwoods, which I should say isn't more than three miles furder."

The arrangement was made, a horse and sleigh ordered, and early in the afternoon we started from Warburton.

The sleighing was good, but the same could not be said of the horse; he was a big roan, powerful and steady, but entirely too deliberate in action. Uncle Beamish, however, was quite satisfied with him.

"What you want when you are going to take a journey with a horse," said he, "is stayin' power. Your fast trotter is all very well for a mile or two, but if I have got to go into the country in winter, give me a horse like this."

I did not agree with him, but we jogged along quite pleasantly until the afternoon grew prematurely dark and it began to snow.

"Now," said I, giving the roan a useless

cut, "what we ought to have is a fast horse, so that we may get there before there is a storm."

"No, Doctor, you're wrong," said Uncle Beamish. "What we want is a strong horse that will take us there whether it storms or not, and we have got him. And who cares for a little snow that won't hurt nobody."

, I did not care for snow, and we turned up our collars and went as merrily as people can go to the music of slowly jingling sleigh-bells.

The snow began to fall rapidly, and, what was worse, the wind blew directly in our faces, so that sometimes my eyes were so plastered up with snow-flakes that I could scarcely see how to drive. I never knew snow to fall with such violence ; the roadway in front of us, as far as I could see it, was soon one unbroken stretch of white from fence to fence.

"This is the big storm of the season," said Uncle Beamish, "and it is a good thing we started in time, for if the wind keeps blowin', this road will be pretty hard to travel in a couple of hours."

In about half an hour the wind lulled a lit-

SHE MADE BUT A STEP INTO THE ROOM AND STOOD HOLDING THE DOOR.

tle and I could get a better view of our surroundings, although I could not see very far
through the swiftly descending snow.

"I was thinkin'," said Uncle Beamish,
"that it might be a good idee, when we get
to Crocker's place, to stop a little, and let
you warm your fingers and nose. Crocker's
is ruther more than half-way to the pike."

"Oh, I do not want to stop anywhere,"
I replied, quickly; "I am all right."

Nothing was said for some time and then
Uncle Beamish remarked:

"I don't want to stop any more than you
do, but it does seem strange that we ain't
passed Crocker's yit; we could hardly miss
his house, it is so close to the road. This
horse is slow, but I tell you one thing, Doctor, he's improvin'; he is goin' better than he
did. That's the way with this kind; it takes
them a good while to get warmed up, but they
keep on gettin' fresher instead of tireder."

The big roan was going better, but still we
did not reach Crocker's, which disappointed
Uncle Beamish, who wanted to be assured
that the greater part of his journey was over.

"We must have passed it," he said, " when
the snow was so blindin'."

I did not wish to discourage him by saying that I did not think we had yet reached Crocker's, but I believed I had a much better appreciation of our horse's slowness than he had.

Again the wind began to blow in our faces, and the snow fell faster, but the violence of the storm seemed to encourage our horse, for his pace was now greatly increased.

"'That's the sort of beast to have," exclaimed Uncle Beamish, spluttering as the snow blew in his mouth; "he is gettin' his spirits up just when they are most wanted. We must have passed Crocker's a good while ago, and it can't be long before we get to the pike; and it's time we was there, for it's darkenin'.'"

On and on we went, but still we did not reach the pike. We had lost a great deal of time during the first part of the journey and, although the horse was travelling so much better now, his pace was below the average of good roadsters.

"When we get to the pike," said Uncle Beamish, "you can't miss it, for this road doesn't cross it; all you've got to do is to turn to the left, and in ten minutes you will see the lights in my sister's house; and I'll tell you, Doctor, if you would like to stop there for the night, she'd be mighty glad to have you."

"Much obliged," replied I, "but I shall go on; it's not late yet, and I can reach the Collingwoods in good time."

We now drove on in silence, our horse actually arching his neck as he thumped through the snow. Drifts had begun to form across the road, but through these he bravely plunged.

"Stayin' power is what we want, Doctor," exclaimed Uncle Beamish; "where would your fast trotter be in drifts like these, I'd like to know? We got the right horse when we got this one, but I wish we had been goin' this fast all the time."

It grew darker and darker, but at last we saw not far in front of us a light.

"That beats me," said Uncle Beamish, "I don't remember no other house so near the road. It can't be we ain't passed Crocker's yit. If we ain't got no furder than that, I'm in favor of stoppin'. I'm not afraid of a snowstorm, but I ain't a fool nuther, and if we haven't got furder than Crocker's it will be foolhardy to try to push on through the dark and these big drifts which will be gettin' bigger."

I did not give it up so easily. I greatly wished to reach my destination that night. But there were three wills in the party, and one of them belonged to the horse. Before I had any idea of such a thing the animal made a sudden turn, too sudden for safety, passed through a wide gateway, and after a few rapid bounds which, to my surprise, I could not restrain, he stopped suddenly.

"Hello!" exclaimed Uncle Beamish, peering forward, "here's a barn-door," and he immediately began to throw off the fur robe that covered our knees.

"What are you going to do?" I asked.

"I'm goin' to open the barn-door and let the horse go in," said he, "he seems to want to. I don't know whether this is Crocker's barn or not; it don't look like it, but I may be mistaken. Anyway we will let the horse in and then go to the house. This ain't no night to be travellin' any furder, Doctor, and that is the long and the short of it. If the people here ain't Crockers, I guess they are Christians!"

I had not much time to consider the situation, for while he had been speaking, Uncle Beamish had waded through the snow, and finding the barn-door unfastened had slid it to one side. Instantly the horse entered the dark barn, fortunately finding nothing in his way.

"Now," said Uncle Beamish, "if we can get somethin' to tie him with, so that he don't do no mischief, we can leave him here and go up to the house."

I carried a pocket lantern, and quickly lighted it.

"By George!" said Uncle Beamish, as I held up the lantern, "this ain't much of a barn, it's no more than a wagon-house; it ain't Crocker's—but no matter—we'll go up to the house. Here is a hitchin' rope."

We fastened the horse, threw a robe over him, shut the barn-door behind us, and slowly made our way to the back of the house in which there was a lighted window. Mounting a little portico we reached a door, and were about to knock, when it was opened for us. A woman, plainly a servant, stood in a kitchen, light and warm.

"Come right in," she said, "I heard your

bells. Did you put your horse in the barn?"

"Yes," said Uncle Beamish, "and now we would like to see——"

"All right," interrupted the woman, moving toward an inner door. "Just wait here for a minute; I'm going up to tell her."

"I don't know this place," said Uncle Beamish, as we stood by the kitchen stove, "but I expect it belongs to a widow woman."

"What makes you think that?" I asked.

"'Cause she said she was goin' to tell *her*. If there had been a man in the house she would have gone to tell *him*."

In a few moments the woman returned.

"She says you are to take off your wet things and then go into the sitting-room. She'll be down in a minute."

I looked at Uncle Beamish, thinking it was his right to make explanations, but, giving me a little wink, he began to take off his overcoat. It was plain to perceive that Uncle Beamish desired to assume that a place of refuge would be offered us.

"It's an awful bad night," he said to the woman, as he sat down to take off his Arctic overshoes.

"It's all that," said she. "You may hang your coats over them chairs; it won't matter if they do drip on this bare floor. Now, then, come right into the sitting-room."

In spite of my disappointment I was glad to be in a warm house, and hoped we might be able to stay there. I could hear the storm beating furiously against the window-panes behind the drawn shades. There was a stove in the sitting-room and a large lamp.

"Sit down," said the woman, "she will be here in a minute."

"It strikes me," said Uncle Beamish, when we were left alone, "that somebody is expected in this house, most likely to spend Christmas, and that we are mistook for them, whoever they are."

"I have the same idea," I replied, "and we must explain as soon as possible."

"Of course we will do that," said he, "but I can tell you one thing: whoever is expected ain't comin', for they can't get here. But we've got to stay here to-night, no matter who comes or doesn't come, and we've got to be keerful in speaking to the woman of the house. If she is one kind of a person we can offer to pay for lodgin's and horse-feed; but if she is another kind, we must steer clear of mentionin' pay, for it will make her angry. You had better leave the explainin' business to me."

I was about to reply that I was more than willing to do so, when the door opened and a person entered—evidently the mistress of the house. She was tall and thin, past middle age, and plainly dressed. Her pale countenance wore a defiant look, and behind her spectacles blazed a pair of dark eyes, which, after an instant's survey of her visitors, were fixed steadily upon me. She made but a step into the room, and stood holding the door. We both rose from our chairs.

" You can sit down again," she said sharply to me, "I don't want you. Now, sir," she continued, turning to Uncle Beamish, "please come with me."

Uncle Beamish gave a glance of surprise at me, but he immediately followed the old lady out of the room, and the door was closed behind them.

For ten minutes, at least, I sat quietly waiting to see what would happen next; very much surprised at the remark that had been made to me, and wondering at Uncle Beamish's protracted absence. Suddenly he entered the room and closed the door.

"Here's a go," said he, slapping his leg, but very gently; "we're mistook the worst kind; we're mistook for doctors."

"That is only half a mistake," said I. "What is the matter, and what can I do?"

"Nothin'," said he, quickly, "that is, nothin' your own self. Just the minute she got me outside that door she began pitchin' into you. 'I suppose that's young Dr. Glover,' said she. I told her it was, and then she went on to say, givin' me no chance to explain nothin', that she didn't want to have anything to do with you, that she thought it was a shame to turn people's houses into paupers' hospitals for the purpose of teaching medical students; that she had heard of you, and what she had heard she hadn't liked. All this time she kept goin' upstairs and I follerin' her, and the fust thing I knowed she opened a door and went into a room, and I went in after her, and there, in a bed, was a patient of some kind. I was tuk back dreadful, for the state of the case came to me like a flash. Your uncle had been sent for and I was mistook for him. Now, what to say was a puzzle to me, and I began to think pretty fast. It was an awkward business to have to explain things to that sharp-set old woman. The fact is I didn't know how to begin, and was a good deal afraid besides, but she didn't give me no time for considerin'. 'I think it's her brain,' said she, 'but perhaps you'll know better. Catherine, uncover your head!' and with that the patient turned over a little and uncovered her head, which she had had the sheet over. It was a young woman, and she gave me a good look, but she didn't say nothin'. Now I *was* in a state of mind."

"Of course you must have been," I answered. "Why didn't you tell her that you were not a doctor, but that I was. It would have been easy enough to explain matters ; she might have thought my uncle could not come and he had sent me, and that you had come along for company. The patient ought to be attended to without delay."

"She's got to be attended to," said Uncle Beamish, "or else there will be a row and we'll have to travel—storm or no storm. But if you had heard what that old woman said about young doctors, and you in particular, you would know that you wasn't goin' to have

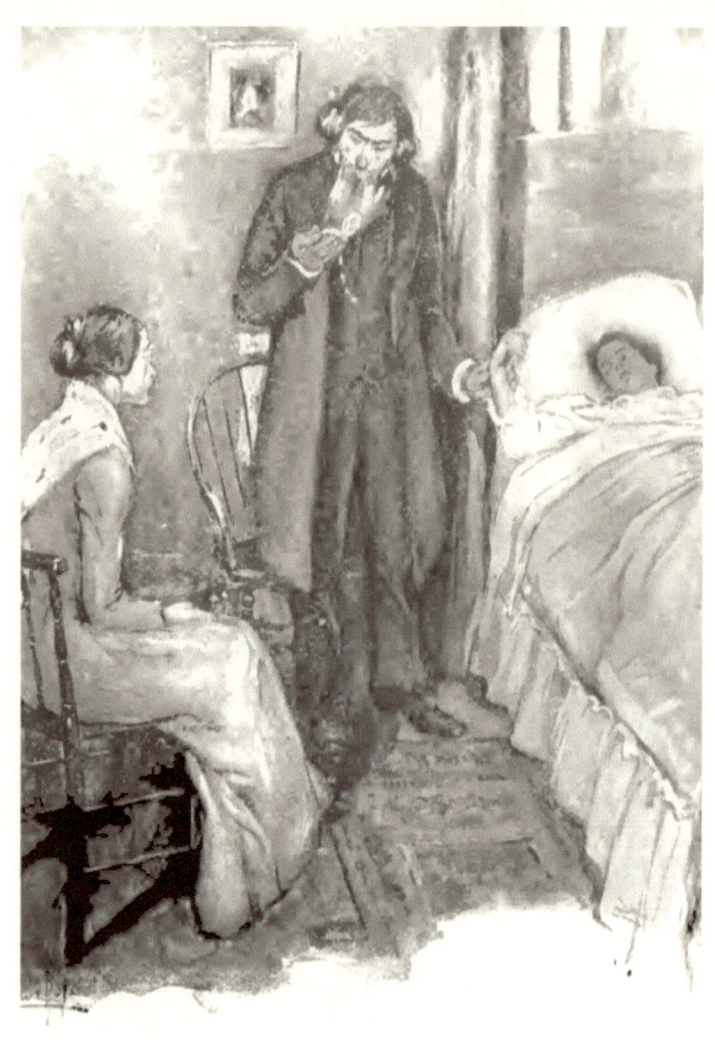

"I HAD NOTHING TO DO BUT STEP UP AND FEEL HER PULSE."

anything to do with this case, at least you
wouldn't show in it. But I've got no more time
for talkin'; I came down here on business.
When the old lady said 'Catherine, hold out
your hand!' and she held it out, I had nothin'
to do but step up and feel her pulse. I know
how to do that, for I have done a lot of
nussin' in my life, and then it seemed nat'ral
to ask her to put out her tongue, and when
she did it I gave a look at it and nodded my
head. 'Do you think it is her brain?' said
the old woman, half whisperin'. 'Can't say
anything about that yit,' said I, 'I must go
downstairs and get the medicine-case. The
fust thing to do is to give her a draught, and
I will bring it up to her as soon as it is mixed.'
You have got a pocket medicine-case with
you, haven't you?"

"Oh, yes," said I, "it is in my overcoat."

"I knowed it," said Uncle Beamish. "An
old doctor might go visitin' without his medicine-case, but a young one would be sure to
take it along, no matter where he was goin'.
Now you get it, please, quick."

"My notion is," said he, when I returned
from the kitchen with the case, "that you mix
somethin' that might soothe her a little, if she

has got anything the matter with her brain, and which won't hurt her if she hasn't; and then, when I take it up to her, you tell me what symptoms to look for. I can do it, I have spent nights looking for symptoms. Then, when I come down and report, you might send her up somethin' that would keep her from gettin' any wuss till the doctor can come in the mornin', for he ain't comin' here to-night."

"A very good plan," said I. "Now, what can I give her? What is the patient's age?"

"Oh, her age don't matter much," said Uncle Beamish, impatiently; "she may be twenty, more or less, and any mild stuff will do to begin with."

"I will give her some sweet spirits of nitre," said I, taking out a little vial. "Will you ask the servant for a glass of water and a teaspoon?"

"Now," said I, when I had quickly prepared the mixture, "she can have a teaspoonful of this and another in ten minutes, and then we will see whether we will go on with it or not."

"And what am I to look for?" said he.

"In the first place," said I, producing a

clinical thermometer, "you must take her temperature ; you know how to do that ?"

"Oh, yes," said he, "I have done it hundreds of times; she must hold it in her mouth five minutes."

"Yes, and while you are waiting," I continued, "you must try to find out, in the first place, if there are, or have been, any signs of delirium. You might ask the old lady, and besides, you may be able to judge for yourself."

"I can do that," said he, "I have seen lots of it."

"Then, again," said I, "you must observe whether or not her pupils are dilated ; you might also inquire whether there had been any partial paralysis or numbness in any part of the body ; these things must be looked for in brain trouble. Then you can come down, ostensibly to prepare another prescription, and when you have reported, I have no doubt I can give you something which will modify, or I should say——"

"Hold her where she is till mornin'," said Uncle Beamish ; "that's what you mean. Be quick ; give me that thermometer and the tumbler, and when I come down again, I reckon you can fit her out with a prescription just as good as anybody."

He hurried away and I sat down to consider. I was full of ambition, full of enthusiasm for the practice of my profession. I would have been willing to pay largely for the privilege of undertaking an important case, by myself, in which it would depend upon me whether or not I should call in a consulting brother. So far, in the cases I had undertaken, a consulting brother had always called himself in ; that is, I had practised in hospitals or with my uncle. Perhaps it might be found necessary, notwithstanding all that had been said against me, that I should go up to take charge of this case. I wished I had not forgotten to ask the old man how he had found the tongue and pulse.

In less than a quarter of an hour Uncle Beamish returned.

"Well," said I, quickly, "what are the symptoms ? "

"I'll give them to you," said he, taking his seat. "I'm not in such a hurry now, because I told the old woman I would like to wait a little and see how that fust medicine acted. The patient spoke to me this time ; when I took the thermometer out of her mouth she says, 'You are comin' up agin, Doctor?' speaking low and quickish, as if she wanted nobody but me to hear."

"But how about the symptoms?" said I, impatiently.

"Well," he answered, "in the fust place her temperature is ninety-eight and a half, and that's about nat'ral, I take it."

"Yes," I said, "but you didn't tell me about her tongue and pulse."

"There wasn't nothin' remarkable about them," said he.

"All of which means," I remarked, "that there is no fever; but that is not at all a necessary accompaniment of brain derangements. How about the dilatation of her pupils?"

"There isn't none," said Uncle Beamish, "they are ruther squinched up if anything; and as to delirium, I couldn't see no signs of it, and when I asked the old lady about the numbness, she said she didn't believe there had been any."

"No tendency to shiver, no disposition to stretch?"

"No," said the old man, "no chance for quinine."

"The trouble is," said I, standing before the stove and fixing my mind upon the case with earnest intensity, "that there are so few symptoms in brain derangement. If I could only get hold of something tangible——"

"If I was you," interrupted Uncle Beamish, "I wouldn't try to get hold of nothin'. I would just give her somethin' to keep her where she is till mornin'. If you can do that, I'll guarantee that any good doctor can take her up and go on with her to-morrow."

Without noticing the implication contained in these remarks, I continued my consideration of the case.

"If I could get a drop of her blood," said I.

"No, no!" exclaimed Uncle Beamish, "I'm not goin' to do anything of that sort. What in the name of common sense would you do with her blood?"

"I would examine it microscopically," I said. "I might find out all I want to know."

Uncle Beamish did not sympathize with this method of diagnosis.

"If you did find out there was the wrong kind of germs, you couldn't do anything with them to-night, and it would just worry you," said the old man. "I believe that nature will git along fust rate without any help, at least till mornin'. But you've got to give her some medicine, not so much for her good as for our good. If she's not treated we're bounced. Can't you give her somethin' that would do anybody good, no matter what's the matter with 'em? If it was the spring of the year I would say sarsaparilla. If you could mix her up somethin' and put it into some of them benevolent microbes the doctors talk about, it would be a good deed to do to anybody."

"The benign bacilli," said I; "unfortunately I haven't any of them with me."

"And if you had," he remarked, "I'd be in favor of givin' 'em to the old woman. I take it they would do her more good than anybody else. Come along now, Doctor, it is about time for me to go upstairs and see how the other stuff acted—not on the patient, I don't mean, but on the old woman. The fact is, you know, it's her we're dosin'."

"Not at all," said I, speaking a little severely, "I am trying to do my very best for the patient, but I fear I cannot do it without seeing her. Don't you think that if you told the old lady how absolutely necessary——"

"Don't say anything more about that," exclaimed Uncle Beamish. "I hoped I wouldn't have to mention it, but she told me agin that she would never have one of those unfledged medical students, just out of the egg-shell, experimentin' on any of her family, and from what she said about you in particular, I should say she considered you as a medical chick without even down on you."

"What can she know of me?" I asked, indignantly.

"Give it up," said he, "can't guess it; but that ain't the pint—the pint is, what are you goin' to give her? When I was young the doctors used to say, when you are in doubt, give calomel, as if you were playin' trumps."

"Nonsense, nonsense," said I, my eyes earnestly fixed upon my open medical case.

"I suppose a mustard plaster on the back of her neck——"

"Wouldn't do at all," I interrupted. "Wait a minute now—yes—I know what I will do, I will give her sodium bromide, ten grains."

"'Which will hit if it's a deer and miss if it's a calf,' as the hunter said?" inquired Uncle Beamish.

"It will certainly not injure her," said I,

"and I am quite sure it will be a positive advantage. If there has been cerebral disturbance, which has subsided temporarily, it will assist her to tide over the interim before its recurrence."

"All right," said Uncle Beamish, "give it to me and I'll be off; it's time I showed up agin."

He did not stay upstairs very long, this time.

"No symptoms yit, but the patient looked at me as if she wanted to say somethin', but she didn't git no chance, for the old lady set herself down as if she was planted in a garden-bed and intended to stay there; but the patient took the medicine as mild as a lamb."

"That is very good," said I. "It may be that she appreciates the seriousness of her case better than we do."

"I should say she wants to git well," he replied, "she looks like that sort of a person to me. The old woman said she thought we would have to stay awhile till the storm slackened, and I said, yes, indeed, and there wasn't any chance of its slackenin' to-night; besides, I wanted to see the patient before bedtime."

At this moment the door opened and the servant woman came in.

"She says you are to have supper, and it will be ready in about half an hour. One of you had better go out and attend to your horse, for the man is not coming back to-night."

"I will go to the barn," said I, rising. Uncle Beamish also rose and said he would go with me.

"I guess you can find some hay and oats," said the woman, as we were putting on our coats and overshoes in the kitchen, "and here's a lantern. We don't keep no horse now, but there's feed left."

As we pushed through the deep snow into the barn, Uncle Beamish said :

"I've been tryin' my best to think where we are, without askin' any questions, and I'm dead beat ; I don't remember no such house as this on the road."

"Perhaps we got off the road," said I.

"That may be," said he as we entered the barn ; "it's a straight road from Warburton to the pike near my sister's house, but there's two other roads that branch off to the right and strike the pike furder off to the east; perhaps we got on one of them in all that darkness and perplexing whiteness, when it wasn't easy to see whether we were keepin' a straight road or not."

The horse neighed as we approached with a light.

" I would not be at all surprised," said I, " if this horse had once belonged here and that was the reason why, as soon as he got a chance, he turned and made straight for his old home."

" That isn't unlikely," said Uncle Beamish, " and that's the reason we did not pass Crocker's. But here we are, wherever it is, and here we've got to stay till mornin'."

We found hay and oats and a pump in the corner of the wagon-house, and, having put the horse in the stall and made him as comfortable as possible with some old blankets, we returned to the house, bringing our valises with us.

Our supper was served in the sitting-room because there was a good fire there, and the servant told us we would have to eat by ourselves, as she was not coming down.

" We'll excuse her," said Uncle Beamish, with an alacrity of expression that might have caused suspicion.

We had a good supper, and were then shown a room on the first floor on the other side of the hall, where the servant said we were to sleep.

We sat by the stove awhile, waiting for developments, but, as Uncle Beamish's bed-time was rapidly approaching, he sent word to the sick-chamber that he was coming up for his final visit.

This time he stayed upstairs but a few minutes.

"She's fast asleep," said he, "and the old woman says she'll call me if I'm needed in the night, and you'll have to jump up sharp and overhaul that medicine case, if that happens."

The next morning, and very early in the morning, I was awaked by Uncle Beamish, who stood at my side.

"Look here," said he, I've been outside : it's stopped snowin' and it's clearin' off. I've been to the barn and I've fed the horse, and I tell you what I'm in favor of doin'. There's nobody up yit and I don't want to stay here and make no explanations to that old woman. I don't fancy gettin' into rows on Christmas mornin'. We've done all the good we can here, and the best thing we can do now is to get away before anybody is up and leave a note sayin' that we've got to go on without losing time, and that we will send another doctor as soon as possible. My sister's doctor don't live fur away from her, and I know she will be willin' to send for him. Then our duty will be done, and what the old woman thinks of us won't make no difference to nobody."

"That plan suits me," said I, rising; "I don't want to stay here and, as I am not to be allowed to see the patient, there is no reason why I should stay. What we have done will more than pay for our supper and lodgings, so that our consciences are clear."

"But you must write a note," said Uncle Beamish. "Got any paper?"

I tore a leaf from my note-book and went to the window, where it was barely light enough for me to see how to write.

"Make it short," said the old man, "I'm awful fidgetty to get off."

I made it very short, and then, valises in hand, we quietly took our way to the kitchen.

"How this floor does creak!" said Uncle Beamish. "Get on your overcoat and shoes

as quick as you can, and we will leave the
note on this table.''

I had just shaken myself into my overcoat
when Uncle Beamish gave a subdued excla-
mation, and quickly turning, I saw entering
the kitchen, a female figure in winter wraps
and carrying a hand-bag.

"By George!" whispered the old man,
"it's the patient!"

The figure advanced directly toward me.

"Oh, Dr. Glover!" she whispered, "I am
so glad to get down before you went away."

I stared in amazement at the speaker, but
even in the dim light I recognized her. This
was the human being whose expected presence
at the Collingwood mansion was taking me
there to spend Christmas.

"Kitty!" I exclaimed—"Miss Burroughs,
I mean—what is the meaning of this?"

"Don't ask me for any meanings now," she
said, "I want you and your uncle to take me
to the Collingwoods. I suppose you are on your
way there, for they wrote you were coming
—and, oh! let us be quick, for I'm afraid
Jane will come down and she will be sure to
wake up Aunty. I saw one of you go out to
the barn and knew you intended to leave, so

I got ready just as fast as I could. But I must leave some word for Aunty."

"I have written a note," said I. "But are you well enough to travel?"

"Just let me add a line to it," said she; "I am as well as ever I was."

I gave her a pencil and she hurriedly wrote something on the paper which I had left on the kitchen-table. Then, quickly glancing around, she picked up a large carving-fork and, sticking it through the paper into the soft wood of the table, she left it standing there.

"Now it won't blow away when we open the door," she whispered. "Come on."

"You cannot go out to the barn," I said, "we will bring up the sleigh."

"Oh, no, no, no," she answered, "I must not wait here. If I once get out of the house I shall feel safe. Of course I shall go, any-way, but I don't want any quarrelling on this Christmas morning."

"I'm with you there," said Uncle Beamish, approvingly. "Doctor, we can take her to the barn without her touching the snow. Let her sit in this arm-chair, and we can carry her between us. She's no weight."

In half a minute the kitchen door was softly closed behind us and we were carrying Miss Burroughs to the barn. My soul was in a wild tumult; dozens of questions were on my tongue, but I had no chance to ask any of them.

Uncle Beamish and I returned to the porch for the valises, and then, closing the back door, we rapidly began to make preparations for leaving.

"I suppose," said Uncle Beamish, as we went into the stable, leaving Miss Burroughs in the wagon-house, "that this business is all right? You seem to know the young woman, and she is of age to act for herself."

"Whatever she wants to do," I answered, "is perfectly right; you may trust to that. I do not understand the matter any more than you do, but I know she is expected at the Collingwoods and wants to go there."

"Very good," said Uncle Beamish, "we'll get away fust and ask explanations afterward."

"Doctor Glover," said Miss Burroughs as we led the horse into the wagon-house, "don't put the bells on him; stuff them gently under the seat, as softly as you can. But how are we all to go away? I have been looking at that sleigh, and it is intended only for two."

"It's rather late to think of that, Miss," said Uncle Beamish, "but there's one thing that's certain. We're both very polite to ladies, but neither of us is willin' to be left behind on this trip. But it's a good-sized sleigh and we'll all pack in, well enough. You and me can sit on the back seat, and the Doctor can stand up in front of us and drive. In old times it was considered the right thing for the driver of the sleigh to stand up and do his drivin'."

The baggage was carefully stowed away, and, after a look around the dimly lighted wagon-house, Miss Burroughs and Uncle Beamish got into the sleigh and I tucked the big fur-robe around them.

"I hate to make a journey before breakfast," said Uncle Beamish, as I was doing this, "especially on Christmas mornin', but somehow or other there seems to be somethin' jolly about this business, and we won't have to wait so long for breakfast nuther. It can't be far from my sister's, and we'll all stop there and have breakfast; then you two can leave me and go on. She'll be as glad to

see any friends of mine as if they were her
own. And she'll be pretty sure, on a mornin'
like this, to have buckwheat cakes and sausages."

Miss Burroughs looked at the old man with
a puzzled air, but she asked him no questions.

" How are you going to keep yourself warm,
Dr. Glover ? " she said.

" Oh, this long ulster will be enough for
me," I replied, "and as I shall stand up, I
could not use a robe if we had another."

In fact, the thought of being with Miss
Burroughs and the anticipation of a sleigh-
ride alone with her, after we had left Uncle
Beamish with his sister, had put me into
such a glow that I scarcely knew it was cold
weather.

" You'd better be keerful, Doctor," said
Uncle Beamish ; " you don't want to git rheu-
matism in your jints on this Christmas mornin'. Here's this horse-blanket that we are
settin' on ; we don't need it and you'd better
wrap it round you, after you get in, to keep
your legs warm."

" Oh, do ! " said Miss Burroughs, " it may
look funny, but we will not meet anybody so
early as this."

"All right!" said I, "and now we are ready to start."

I slid back the barn-door and then led the horse outside. Closing the door, and making as little noise as possible in doing it, I got into the sleigh, finding plenty of room to stand up in front of my companions. Now I wrapped the horse-blanket about the lower part of my body, and, as I had no belt with which to secure it, Miss Burroughs kindly offered to fasten it round my waist by means of a long pin which she took from her hat. It is impossible to describe the exhilaration that pervaded me as she performed this kindly office. After thanking her warmly, I took the reins and we started.

"It is so lucky," whispered Miss Burroughs, "that I happened to think about the bells. We don't make any noise at all."

This was true; the slowly uplifted hoofs of the horse descended quietly into the soft snow, and the sleigh-runners slipped along without a sound.

"Drive straight for the gate, Doctor," whispered Uncle Beamish, "it don't matter nothin, about goin' over flower-beds and grass-plats in such weather."

I followed his advice, for no roadway could be seen. But we had gone but a short distance when the horse suddenly stopped.

"What's the matter?" asked Miss Burroughs, in a low voice. "Is it too deep for him?"

"We're in a drift," said Uncle Beamish. "But it's not too deep; make him go ahead, Doctor."

I clicked gently and tapped the horse with the whip, but he did not move.

"What a dreadful thing," whispered Miss Burroughs, leaning forward, "for him to stop so near the house. Doctor Glover, what does this mean?" and, as she spoke, she half rose behind me. "Where did Sir Rohan come from?"

"Who's he?" asked Uncle Beamish, quickly.

"That horse," she answered. "That's my aunt's horse; she sold him a few days ago."

"By George!" ejaculated Uncle Beamish, unconsciously raising his voice a little, "Wilson bought him, and his bringin' us here is as plain as a-b-c. And now he don't want to leave home."

"But he has got to do it," said I, jerking

the horse's head to one side and giving him a
cut with the whip.

"Don't whip him," whispered Miss Burroughs, "it always makes him more stubborn.
How glad I am I thought of the bells! The
only way to get him to go is to mollify him."

"But how is that to be done?" I asked,
anxiously.

"You must give him sugar and pat his
neck. If I had some sugar and could get
out——"

"But you haven't it, and you can't get out,"
said Uncle Beamish. "Try him again, Doctor!"

I jerked the reins impatiently. "Go
along!" said I, but he did not go along.

"Haven't you got somethin' in your medicine-case you could mollify him with?" said
Uncle Beamish. "Somethin' sweet that he
might like?"

For an instant I caught at this absurd suggestion, and my mind ran over the contents
of my little bottles. If I had known his
character, some sodium bromide in his morning feed might, by this time, have mollified
his obstinacy.

"If I could be free of this blanket," said I,

fumbling at the pin behind me, "I would get out and lead him into the road."

"You could not do it," said Miss Burroughs. "You might pull his head off, but he wouldn't move; I have seen him tried."

At this moment a window-sash in the second story of the house was raised, and there, not thirty feet from us, stood an elderly female, wrapped in a gray shawl, with piercing eyes shining through great spectacles.

"You seem to be stuck," said she, sarcastically. "You are worse stuck than the fork was in my kitchen-table."

We made no answer. I do not know how Miss Burroughs looked or felt, or what was the appearance of Uncle Beamish, but I know I must have been very red in the face. I gave the horse a powerful crack and shouted to him to go on; there was no need for low speaking now.

"You needn't be cruel to dumb animals," said the old lady, "and you can't budge him. He never did like snow, especially in going away from home. You cut a powerful queer figure, young man, with that horse-blanket around you. You don't look much like **a** practising physician."

"YOU CUT A POWERFUL QUEER FIGURE, YOUNG MAN."

"Miss Burroughs," I exclaimed, "please take that pin out of this blanket. If I can get at his head I know I can pull him around and make him go."

But she did not seem to hear me. "Aunty," she cried, "it's a shame to stand there and make fun of us. We have got a perfect right to go away if we want to, and we ought not to be laughed at."

The old lady paid no attention to this remark.

"And there's that false doctor," she said; "I wonder how he feels just now."

"False doctor!" exclaimed Miss Burroughs, "I don't understand."

"Young lady," said Uncle Beamish, "I'm no false doctor. I intended to tell you all about it as soon as I got a chance, but I haven't had one. And, old lady, I'd like you to know that I don't say I'm a doctor, but I do say I'm a nuss, and a good nuss, and you can't deny it."

To this challenge the figure at the window made no answer.

"Catherine," said she, "I can't stand here and take cold, but I just want to know one thing. Have you positively made up your mind to marry that young doctor in the horse-blanket ? "

This question fell like a bomb-shell into the middle of the stationary sleigh.

I had never asked Kitty to marry me. I loved her with all my heart and soul, and I hoped, almost believed, that she loved me. It had been my intention, when we should be left together in the sleigh this morning, after dropping Uncle Beamish at his sister's house, to ask her to marry me.

The old woman's question pierced me as if it had been a flash of lightning, coming through the frosty air of a winter morning. I dropped the useless reins and turned. Kitty's face was ablaze ; she made a movement as if she was about to jump out of the sleigh and flee.

"Oh, Kitty ! " said I, bending down toward her, " tell her yes, I beg, I entreat, I implore you to tell her yes ! Oh, Kitty ! if you don't say yes I shall never know another happy day."

For one moment Kitty looked up into my face, and then said she :

"It is my positive intention to marry him."

With the agility of a youth, Uncle Beamish threw the robe from him and sprang out into the deep snow; then turning toward us, he took off his hat.

"By George!" said he, "you're a pair of trumps. I never did see any human bein's step up to the mark more prompt. Madam," he cried, addressing the old lady, "you ought to be the proudest woman in this county at seein' such a thing as this happen under your window of a Christmas mornin'. And now the best thing that you can do is to invite us all in to have breakfast."

"You'll have to come in," said she, "or else stay out there and freeze to death, for that horse isn't going to take you away. And if my niece really intends to marry the young man and has gone so far as to start to run away with him—and with a false doctor—of course I've got no more to say about it, and you can come in and have breakfast;" and with that she shut down the window.

"That's talkin'," said Uncle Beamish. "Sit still, Doctor, and I'll lead him around to the back door. I guess he'll move quick enough when you want him to turn back."

Without the slightest objection Sir Rohan

permitted himself to be turned back and led
up to the kitchen porch.

"Now you two sparklin' angels get out,"
said Uncle Beamish, "and go in.   I'll attend
to the horse."

Jane, with a broad grin on her face, opened
the kitchen door.

"Merry Christmas to you both!" said she.

"Merry Christmas!" we cried, and each of
us shook her by the hand.

"Go in the sitting-room and get warm,"
said Jane, "She'll be down pretty soon."

I do not know how long we were together
in that sitting-room.   We had thousands of
things to say, and we said most of them.
Among other things we managed to get in
some explanations of the occurrences of the
previous night.   Kitty told her tale briefly.
She and her aunt, to whom she was making
a visit, and who wanted her to make her house
her home, had had a quarrel two days before.
Kitty was wild to go to the Collingwoods, and
the old lady, who, for some reason, hated the
family, was determined she should not go.
But Kitty was immovable and never gave up
until she found that her aunt had gone so far
as to dispose of her horse, thus making it im-

possible to travel in such weather, there being no public conveyances passing the house. Kitty was an orphan, and had a guardian who would have come to her aid, but she could not write to him in time, and, in utter despair, she went to bed. She would not eat or drink, she would not speak, and she covered up her head.

"After a day and a night," said Kitty, " Aunty got dreadfully frightened and thought something was the matter with my brain ; her family are awfully anxious about their brains. I knew she had sent for the doctor, and I was glad of it, for I thought he would help me. I must say I was surprised when I first saw that Mr. Beamish, for I thought he was Doctor Morris. Now tell me about your coming here."

"And so," she said, when I had finished, " you had no idea that you were prescribing for me ! Please do tell me what were those medicines you sent up to me and which I took like a truly good girl."

"I didn't know it at the time," said I, " but I sent you sixty drops of the deepest, strongest love in a glass of water, and ten grains of perfect adoration."

"Nonsense!" said Kitty, with a blush, and at that moment Uncle Beamish knocked at the door.

"I thought I'd just step in and tell you," said he, "that breakfast will be comin' along in a minute. I found they were going to have buckwheat cakes, anyway, and I prevailed on Jane to put sausages in the bill of fare. Merry Christmas to you both! I would like to say more, but here comes the old lady and Jane."

The breakfast was a strange meal, but a very happy one. The old lady was very dignified; she made no allusion to Christmas or to what had happened, but talked to Uncle Beamish about people in Warburton.

I have a practical mind and, in spite of the present joy, I could not help feeling a little anxiety about what was to be done when breakfast was over; but just as we were about to rise from the table we were all startled by a great jingle of sleigh-bells outside. The old lady arose and stepped to the window.

"There!" said she, turning toward us. "Here's a pretty kettle of fish! There's a two-horse sleigh outside with a man driving and a gentleman in the back seat who I am

JOHN MUST HAVE DRIVEN BACKWARD AND FORWARD
FOR HALF AN HOUR.

sure is Doctor Morris, and he has come all
the way on this bitter cold morning to see
the patient I sent for him to come to. Now,
who is going to tell him he has come on a
fool's errand ? "

" Fool's errand ! " I cried. " Everyone of
you wait in here and I'll go out and tell him."

When I dashed out of doors and stood by
the side of my uncle's sleigh, he was truly an
amazed man.

" I will get in, Uncle," said I, "and if you
will let John drive the horses slowly around
the yard, I will tell you how I happen to be
here."

The story was a much longer one than I
expected it to be, and John must have driven
those horses backward and forward for half
an hour.

" Well," said my uncle at last, " I never saw
your Kitty, but I knew her father and her
mother, and I will go in and take a look at
her. If I like her, I will take you all on to
the Collingwoods and drop Uncle Beamish
at his sister's house."

" I'll tell you what it is, young Doctor,"
said Uncle Beamish at parting, "you ought

to buy that big roan horse; he has been a regular guardian angel to us this Christmas."

"Oh, that would never do at all," cried Kitty. "His patients would all die before he got there."

"That is, if they had anything the matter with them," added my uncle.

THE WIDOW'S CRUISE

THE WIDOW'S CRUISE

THE widow Ducket lived in a small village about ten miles from the New Jersey sea coast. In this village she was born, here she had married and buried her husband, and here she expected somebody to bury her, but she was in no hurry for that, for she had scarcely reached middle age. She was a tall woman with no apparent fat in her composition, and full of activity, both muscular and mental.

She rose at six o'clock in the morning, cooked breakfast, set the table, washed the dishes when the meal was over, milked, churned, swept, washed, ironed, worked in her little garden, attended to the flowers in the front yard, and in the afternoon knitted and quilted and sewed, and after tea she either went to see her neighbors or had them come to see her. When it was really dark she lighted the lamp in her parlor and read for an hour, and if it happened to be one of

Miss Mary Wilkins' books that she read she
expressed doubts as to the realism of the
characters therein described.

These doubts she expressed to Dorcas
Networthy, who was a small, plump woman,
with a solemn face, who had lived with the
widow for many years and who had become
her devoted disciple. Whatever the widow
did that also did Dorcas not so well, for
her heart told her she could never expect to
do that, but with a yearning anxiety to do
everything as well as she could. She rose at
five minutes past six, and in a subsidiary
way she helped to get the breakfast, to eat it,
to wash up the dishes, to work in the garden,
to quilt, to sew, to visit and receive, and no
one could have tried harder than she did to
keep awake when the widow read aloud in
the evening.

All these things happened every day in the
summer time, but in the winter the widow
and Dorcas cleared the snow from their little
front path instead of attending to the flowers,
and in the evening they lighted a fire as well
as a lamp in the parlor.

Sometimes, however, something different
happened, but this was not often, only a few

times in the year. One of the different things occurred when Mrs. Ducket and Dorcas were sitting on their little front porch one summer afternoon, one on the little bench on one side of the door and the other on the little bench on the other side of the door, each waiting, until she should hear the clock strike five, to prepare tea. But it was not yet a quarter to five when a one-horse wagon containing four men came slowly down the street. Dorcas first saw the wagon, and she instantly stopped knitting.

"Mercy on me!" she exclaimed. "Whoever those people are they are strangers here and they don't know where to stop, for they first go to one side of the street and then to the other."

The widow looked around sharply. "Humph!" said she. "Those men are sailor-men. You might see that in a twinkling of an eye. Sailor-men always drive that way because that is the way they sail ships. They first tack in one direction and then in another."

"Mr. Ducket didn't like the sea?" remarked Dorcas, for about the three hundredth time.

"No, he didn't," answered the widow, for
about the two hundred and fiftieth time, for
there had been occasions when she thought
Dorcas put this question inopportunely.
"He hated it, and he was drowned in it
through trusting a sailor-man, which I never
did nor shall. Do you really believe those
people are coming here?"

"Upon my word I do!" said Dorcas, and
her opinion was correct.

The wagon drew up in front of Mrs. Ducket's little white house, and the two women
sat rigidly, their hands in their laps, staring
at the man who drove.

This was an elderly personage with whitish
hair, and under his chin a thin whitish
beard, which waved in the gentle breeze and
gave Dorcas the idea that his head was filled
with hair which was leaking out from below.

"Is this the widow Ducket's?" inquired
this elderly man, in a strong, penetrating
voice.

"That's my name," said the widow, and laying her knitting on the bench beside her she
went to the gate. Dorcas also laid her knitting on the bench beside her and went to the
gate.

" I was told," said the elderly man, " at a house we touched at about a quarter of a mile back, that the widow Ducket's was the only house in this village where there was any chance of me and my mates getting a meal. We are four sailors and we are making from the bay over to Cuppertown, and that's eight miles ahead yet and we are all pretty sharp set for something to eat."

" This is the place," said the widow, " and I do give meals if there is enough in the house and everything comes handy."

" Does everything come handy to-day? " said he.

" It does," said she, " and you can hitch your horse and come in, but I haven't got anything for him."

" Oh, that's all right," said the man, " we brought along stores for him, so we'll just make fast and then come in."

The two women hurried into the house in a state of bustling preparation, for the furnishing of this meal meant one dollar in cash.

The four mariners, all elderly men, descended from the wagon, each one scrambling with alacrity over a different wheel.

A box of broken ship-biscuit was brought

out and put on the ground in front of the horse, who immediately set himself to eating with great satisfaction.

Tea was a little late that day, because there were six persons to provide for instead of two, but it was a good meal, and after the four seamen had washed their hands and faces at the pump in the back yard and had wiped them on two towels furnished by Dorcas, they all came in and sat down. Mrs. Ducket seated herself at the head of the table with the dignity proper to the mistress of the house, and Dorcas seated herself at the other end with the dignity proper to the disciple of the mistress. No service was necessary, for everything that was to be eaten or drunk was on the table.

When each of the elderly mariners had had as much bread and butter, quickly-baked soda biscuit, dried beef, cold ham, cold tongue and preserved fruit of every variety known, as his storage capacity would permit, the mariner in command, Captain Bird, pushed back his chair, whereupon the other mariners pushed back their chairs.

"Madam," said Captain Bird, "we have all made a good meal, which didn't need to be

no better nor more of it, and we're satisfied,
but that horse out there has not had time to
rest himself enough to go the eight miles
that lies ahead of us, so if it's all the same
to you and this good lady, we'd like to sit on
that front porch awhile and smoke our pipes.
I was a-looking at that porch when I came
in, and I bethought to myself what a rare
good place it was to smoke a pipe in."

"There's pipes been smoked there," said
the widow rising, "and it can be done again.
Inside the house I don't allow tobacco, but
on the porch neither of us minds."

So the four Captains betook themselves to
the porch, two of them seating themselves on
the little bench on one side of the door and
two of them on the little bench on the other
side of the door, and lighted their pipes.

"Shall we clear off the table and wash up
the dishes," said Dorcas, "or wait until they
are gone?"

"We will wait until they are gone," said
the widow, "for now that they are here we
might as well have a bit of a chat with them.
When a sailor-man lights his pipe he is generally willing to talk, but when he is eatin'
you can't get a word out of him."

Without thinking it necessary to ask permission, for the house belonged to her, the widow Ducket brought a chair and put it in the hall close to the open front door, and Dorcas brought another chair and seated herself by the side of the widow.

"Do all you sailor-men belong down there at the bay?" asked Mrs. Ducket, and thus the conversation began, and in a few minutes it had reached a point at which Captain Bird thought it proper to say that a great many strange things happen to seamen sailing on the sea which lands-people never dream of.

"Such as anything in particular?" asked the widow, at which remark Dorcas clasped her hands in expectancy.

At this question each of the mariners took his pipe from his mouth and gazed upon the floor in thought.

"There's a good many strange things happened to me and my mates at sea. Would you and that other lady like to hear any of them?" asked Captain Bird.

"We would like to hear them if they are true," said the widow.

"There's nothing happened to me and my mates that isn't true," said Captain Bird, "and here is something that once happened to me: I was on a whaling v'yage when a big sperm whale, just as mad as a fiery bull, came at us, head on, and struck the ship at the stern with such tremendous force that his head crashed right through her timbers and he went nearly half his length into her hull. The hold was mostly filled with empty barrels, for we was just beginning our v'yage, and when he had made kindling wood of these, there was room enough for him. We all expected that it wouldn't take five minutes for the vessel to fill and go to the bottom, and we made ready to take to the boats, but it turned out we didn't need to take to no boats, for as fast as the water rushed into the hold of the ship that whale drank it and squirted it up through the two blow holes in the top of his head, and as there was an open hatchway just over his head the water all went into the sea again, and that whale kept working day and night pumping the water out until we beached the vessel on the island of Trinidad—the whale helping us wonderful on our way over by the powerful working of his tail, which, being outside in the water, acted like a propeller. I don't believe any-

thing stranger than that ever happened to a
whaling ship."

"No," said the widow, "I don't believe
anything ever did."

Captain Bird now looked at Captain Sanderson, and the latter took his pipe out of his
mouth and said that in all his sailing around
the world he had never known anything
queerer than what happened to a big steamship he chanced to be on, which ran into an
island in a fog. Everybody on board thought
the ship was wrecked, but it had twin screws
and was going at such a tremendous speed
that it turned the island entirely upside down
and sailed over it, and he had heard tell that
even now people sailing over the spot could
look down into the water and see the roots
of the trees and the cellars of the houses.

Captain Sanderson now put his pipe back
into his mouth and Captain Burress took out
his pipe.

"I was once in an obelisk ship," said he,
"that used to trade regular between Egypt
and New York carrying obelisks. We had a
big obelisk on board. The way they ship
obelisks is to make a hole in the stern of the
ship and run the obelisk in, p'inted end fore-

THE WIDOW DUCKET SAID NOTHING.

touched the bottom it just stood there, and as
it was such a big obelisk there was about five
and a half feet of it stuck out of the water.
The man who was knocked overboard he just
swum for that obelisk and he climbed up the
hiryglyphics. It was a mighty fine obelisk
and the Egyptians had cut their hiryglyphics
good and deep so that the man could get
hand and foot hold. And when we got to
him and took him off he was sitting high and
dry on the p'inted end of that obelisk. It was
a great pity about the obelisk, for it was a
good obelisk, but as I never heard the company tried to raise it I expect it is standing
there yet."

Captain Burress now put his pipe back into
his mouth and looked at Captain Jenkinson,
who removed his pipe and said :

" The queerest thing that ever happened to
me was about a shark. We was off the Banks
and the time of year was July, and the ice was
coming down and we got in among a lot of it.
Not far away, off our weather bow, there was
a little iceberg which had such a queerness
about it that the Captain and three men went
in a boat to look at it. The ice was mighty
clear ice and you could see almost through it,

and right inside of it, not more than three feet above the water line, and about two feet, or maybe twenty inches, inside the ice, was a whopping big shark, about fourteen feet long —a regular man-eater—frozen in there hard and fast. 'Bless my soul,' said the Captain, 'this is a wonderful curiosity and I'm going to git him out.' Just then one of the men said he saw that shark wink, but the Captain wouldn't believe him, for he said that shark was frozen stiff and hard and couldn't wink. You see the Captain had his own idees about things, and he knew that whales was warm-blooded and would freeze if they was shut up in ice, but he forgot that sharks was not whales and that they're cold-blooded just like toads. And there is toads that has been shut up in rocks for thousands of years, and they stayed alive, no matter how cold the place was, because they was cold-blooded, and when the rocks was split out hopped the frog. But as I said before, the Captain forgot sharks was cold-blooded and he determined to git that one out.

"Now you both know, being housekeepers, that if you take a needle and drive it into a hunk of ice you can split it. The Captain

had a sail-needle with him and so he drove it
into the iceberg right alongside of the shark
and split it. Now the minute he did it he
knew that the man was right when he said
he saw the shark wink, for it flopped out of
that iceberg quicker nor a flash of lightning.

"What a happy fish he must have been!"
ejaculated Dorcas, forgetful of precedent, so
great was her emotion.

"Yes," said Captain Jenkinson, "it was a
happy fish enough, but it wasn't a happy
Captain. You see that shark hadn't had anything to eat, perhaps for a thousand years,
until the Captain came along with his sail-
needle."

"Surely you sailor men do see strange
things," now said the widow, "and the strang-
est thing about them is that they are true."

"Yes, indeed," said Dorcas, "that is the
most wonderful thing."

"You wouldn't suppose," said the widow
Ducket, glancing from one bench of mariners
to the other, "that I have a sea-story to tell,
but I have, and if you like I will tell it to
you."

Captain Bird looked up a little surprised.

" We would like to hear it, indeed we would, madam," said he.

" Aye, aye!" said Captain Burress, and the two other mariners nodded.

" It was a good while ago," she said, " when I was living on the shore near the head of the bay, that my husband was away and I was left alone in the house. One mornin' my sister-in-law, who lived on the other side of the bay, sent me word by a boy on a horse that she hadn't any oil in the house to fill the lamp that she always put in the window to light her husband home, who was a fisherman, and if I would send her some by the boy she would pay me back as soon as they bought oil. The boy said he would stop on his way home and take the oil to her, but he never did stop, or perhaps he never went back, and about five o'clock I began to get dreadfully worried, for I knew if that lamp wasn't in my sister in-law's window by dark she might be a widow before midnight. So I said to myself, 'I've got to get that oil to her, no matter what happens or how it's done.' Of course I couldn't tell what might happen, but there was only one way it could be done, and that was for me to get into the

boat that was tied to the post down by the
water and take it to her, for it was too far
for me to walk around by the head of the
bay.   Now the trouble was I didn't know no
more about a boat and the managin' of it than
any one of you sailor men knows about clear
starchin'.   But there wasn't no use of thinkin'
what I knew and what I didn't know, for I
had to take it to her and there was no way of
doin' it except in that boat.   So I filled a
gallon can, for I thought I might as well take
enough while I was about it, and I went down
to the water and I unhitched that boat and I
put the oil-can into her and then I got in, and
off I started, and when I was about a quarter
of a mile from the shore——"

"Madam," interrupted Captain Bird, "did
you row or—or was there a sail to the boat?"

The widow looked at the questioner for a
moment. "No," said she, "I didn't row.   I
forgot to bring the oars from the house, but
it didn't matter for I didn't know how to use
them, and if there had been a sail I couldn't
have put it up, for I didn't know how to use
it either.   I used the rudder to make the boat
go.   The rudder was the only thing that I
knew anything about.   I'd held a rudder when

I was a little girl and I knew how to work it.
So I just took hold of the handle of the rudder and turned it round and round, and that
made the boat go ahead, you know, and——"

"Madam!" exclaimed Captain Bird, and
the other elderly mariners took their pipes
from their mouths.

"Yes, that is the way I did it," continued
the widow briskly; "big steamships are made
to go by a propeller turning round and round
at their back ends, and I made the rudder
work in the same way, and I got along very
well, too, until suddenly, when I was about a
quarter of a mile from the shore, a most terrible and awful storm arose. There must have
been a typhoon or a cyclone out at sea, for
the waves came up the bay bigger than houses,
and when they got to the head of the bay they
turned around and tried to get out to sea
again; so in this way they continually met,
and made the most awful and roarin' pilin' up
of waves that ever was known.

"My little boat was pitched about as if it
had been a feather in a breeze, and when the
front part of it was cleavin' itself down into
the water the hind part was stickin' up until
the rudder whizzed around like a patent

churn with no milk in it. The thunder began
to roar and the lightnin' flashed, and three
sea-gulls, so nearly frightened to death that
they began to turn up the whites of their
eyes, flew down and sat on one of the seats of
the boat, forgettin' in that awful moment that
man was their nat'ral enemy. I had a couple
of biscuits in my pocket, because I had
thought I might want a bite in crossing, and
I crumbled up one of these and fed the poor
creatures. Then I began to wonder what I
was goin' to do, for things were gettin' awfuller and awfuller every instant, and the little
boat was a-heavin' and a-pitchin' and a-rollin'
and h'istin' itself up, first on one end and then
on the other, to such an extent that if I hadn't
kept tight hold of the rudder handle I'd
slipped off the seat I was sittin' on.

"All of a sudden I remembered that oil in
the can, but just as I was puttin' my fingers
on the cork my conscience smote me. 'Am
I goin' to use this oil,' I said to myself, 'and
let my sister-in-law's husband be wrecked for
want of it?' And then I thought that he
wouldn't want it all that night and perhaps
they would buy oil the next day, and so I
poured out about a tumblerful of it on the

water, and I can just tell you sailor men that
you never saw anything act as prompt as that
did. In three seconds, or perhaps five, the
water all around me, for the distance of a
small front yard, was just as flat as a table and
as smooth as glass, and so invitin' in appearance that the three gulls jumped out of the
boat and began to swim about on it, primin'
their feathers and looking at themselves in
the transparent depths, though I must say
that one of them made an awful face as he
dipped his bill into the water and tasted kerosene.

"Now I had time to sit quiet in the midst
of the placid space I had made for myself and
rest from working of the rudder. Truly it was
a wonderful and marvelous thing to look at.
The waves was roarin' and leapin' up all
around me higher than the roof of this house,
and sometimes their tops would reach over so
that they nearly met and shut out all view of
the stormy sky, which seemed as if it was bein'
torn to pieces by blazin' lightnin', while the
thunder pealed so tremendous that it almost
drowned the roar of the waves. Not only
above and all around me was everything ter-
rific and fearful, but even under me it was the

same, for there was a big crack in the bottom
of the boat as wide as my hand, and through
this I could see down into the water beneath,
and there was——"

"Madam!" ejaculated Captain Bird, the
hand which had been holding his pipe a few
inches from his mouth now dropping to his
knee, and at this motion the hands which held
the pipes of the three other mariners dropped
to their knees.

"Of course it sounds strange," continued
the widow, "but I know that people can see
down into clear water, and the water under
me was clear, and the crack was wide enough
for me to see through, and down under me
was sharks and sword-fishes and other horri-
ble water creatures, which I had never seen
before, all driven into the bay, I haven't a
doubt, by the violence of the storm out at sea.
The thought of my bein' upset and fallin' in
among those monsters made my very blood
run cold, and involuntary-like I began to turn
the handle of the rudder, and in a moment I
shot into a wall of ragin' sea water that was
towerin' around me. For a second I was
fairly blinded and stunned, but I had the cork
out of that oil-can in no time, and very soon,

you'd scarcely believe it if I told you how
soon, I had another placid mill-pond sur-
roundin' of me. I sat there a-pantin' and fan-
nin' with my straw hat, for you'd better believe I was flustered, and then I began to
think how long it would take me to make a
line of mill-ponds clean across the head of
the bay and how much oil it would need and
whether I had enough. So I sat and calculated that if a tumblerful of oil would make a
smooth place about seven yards across, which
I should say was the width of the one I was
in, which I calculated by a measure of my eye
as to how many breadths of carpet it would
take to cover it, and if the bay was two miles
across, betwixt our house and my sister-in-
law's, and although I couldn't get the thing
down to exact figures, I saw pretty soon that
I wouldn't have oil enough to make a level
cuttin' through all those mountainous billows,
and besides, even if I had enough to take me
across, what would be the good of going if
there wasn't any oil left to fill my sister-in-
law's lamp?

"While I was thinkin' and calculatin' a
perfectly dreadful thing happened, which
made me think if I didn't get out of this

pretty soon I'd find myself in a mighty risky
predicament. The oil-can, which I had forgotten to put the cork in, toppled over, and
before I could grab it every drop of the oil
ran into the hind part of the boat, where it
was soaked up by a lot of dry dust that was
there. No wonder my heart sank when I saw
this. Glancin' wildly around me, as people
will do when they are scared, I saw the
smooth place I was in gettin' smaller and
smaller, for the kerosene was evaporatin', as
it will do even off woollen clothes if you give
it time enough. The first pond I had come
out of seemed to be covered up, and the great,
towerin', throbbin' precipice of sea-water was
a-closin' around me.

"Castin' down my eyes in despair I happened to look through the crack in the bottom of the boat, and oh! what a blessed relief it was, for down there everything was
smooth and still, and I could see the sand on
the bottom as level and hard, no doubt, as it
was on the beach. Suddenly the thought
struck me that that bottom would give me
the only chance I had of gettin' out of the
frightful fix I was in. If I could fill that oil-
can with air and then puttin' it under my arm

and takin' a long breath, if I could drop down
on that smooth bottom, I might run along
toward shore, as far as I could, and then,
when I felt my breath was givin' out, I
could take a pull at the oil-can and take another run, and then take another pull and
another run, and perhaps the can would hold
air enough for me until I got near enough to
shore to wade to dry land. To be sure the
sharks and other monsters were down there,
but then they must have been awfully frightened and perhaps they might not remember that man was their nat'ral enemy. Anyway, I thought it would be better to try the
smooth water passage down there than stay
and be swallowed up by the ragin' waves on
top.

"So I blew the can full of air and corked
it, and then I tore up some of the boards
from the bottom of the boat so as to make a
hole big enough for me to get through—and
you sailor men needn't wriggle so when I say
that, for you all know a divin' bell hasn't any
bottom at all and the water never comes in—
and so when I got the hole big enough I took
the oil can under my arm and was just about
to slip down through it when I saw an awful

turtle a-walkin' through the sand at the bottom.   Now, I might trust sharks and swordfishes and sea-serpents to be frightened and forget about their nat'ral enemies, but I never could trust a gray turtle as big as a cart, with a black neck a yard long, with yellow bags to its jaws, to forget anything or to remember anything.   I'd as lieve get into a bath-tub with a live crab as to go down there. It wasn't of no use even so much as thinkin' of it, so I gave up that plan and didn't once look through that hole again."

"And what did you do, madam?" asked Captain Bird, who was regarding her with a face of stone.

"I used electricity," she said.   "Now don't start as if you had a shock of it.   That's what I used.   When I was younger than I was then and sometimes visited friends in the city, we often amused ourselves by rubbing our feet on the carpet until we got ourselves so full of electricity that we could put up our fingers and light the gas.   So I said to myself that if I could get full of electricity for the purpose of lightin' the gas I could get full of it for other purposes, and so, without losin' a moment, I set to work.   I stood up on one of the seats, which was dry, and I rubbed the bottoms of my shoes backward and forward on it with such violence and swiftness that they pretty soon got warm and I began fillin' with electricity, and when I was fully charged with it from my toes to the top of my head I just sprang into the water and swam ashore. Of course I couldn't sink, bein' full of electricity."

Captain Bird heaved a long sigh and rose to his feet, whereupon the other mariners rose to their feet. "Madam," said Captain Bird, "what's to pay for the supper and—the rest of the entertainment?"

"The supper is twenty-five cents apiece," said the widow Ducket, "and everything else is free, gratis."

Whereupon each mariner put his hand into his trousers pocket, pulled out a silver quarter, and handed it to the widow. Then with four solemn "Good-evenin's" they went out to the front gate.

"Cast off, Captain Jenkinson," said Captain Bird, "and you, Captain Burress, clew him up for'ard. You can stay in the bow, Captain Sanderson, and take the sheet lines. I'll go aft."

All being ready, each of the elderly mariners clambered over a wheel, and having seated themselves, they prepared to lay their course for Cuppertown.

But just as they were about to start Captain Jenkinson asked that they lay-to a bit, and clambering down over his wheel, he re-entered the front gate and went up to the door of the house, where the widow and Dorcas were still standing.

"Madam," said he, "I just came back to ask what became of your brother-in-law through his wife's not bein' able to put no light in the window?"

"The storm drove him ashore on our side of the bay," said she, "and the next mornin' he came up to our house and I told him all that had happened to me; and when he took our boat and went home and told that story to his wife she just packed up and went out West, and got divorced from him; and it served him right, too."

"Thank you, ma'am," said Captain Jenkinson, and going out of the gate he clambered up over the wheel and the wagon cleared for Cuppertown.

When the elderly mariners were gone the

widow Ducket, still standing in the door, turned to Dorcas :

"Think of it!" she said, "to tell all that to me, in my own house! And after I had opened my one jar of brandied peaches that I'd been keepin' for special company!"

"In your own house!" ejaculated Dorcas. "And not one of them brandied peaches left!"

The widow jingled the four quarters in her hand before she slipped them into her pocket.

"Anyway, Dorcas," she remarked, "I think we can now say we are square with all the world, and so let's go in and wash the dishes."

"Yes," said Dorcas, "we're square."

LOVE BEFORE BREAKFAST

LOVE BEFORE BREAKFAST

I WAS still a young man when I came into the possession of an excellent estate. This consisted of a large country house, surrounded by lawns, groves, and gardens, and situated not far from the flourishing little town of Boynton. Being an orphan with no brothers or sisters, I set up here a bachelor's hall, in which, for two years, I lived with great satisfaction and comfort, improving my grounds and furnishing my house. When I had made all the improvements which were really needed, and feeling that I now had a most delightful home to come back to, I thought it would be an excellent thing to take a trip to Europe, give my mind a run in fresh fields and pick up a lot of bric-à-brac and ideas for the adornment and advantage of my house and mind.

It was the custom of the residents in my neighborhood who owned houses and travelled in the summer to let their houses during their absence, and my business agent and myself agreed that this would be an excellent thing for me to do. If the house were let to a suitable family it would yield me a considerable income, and the place would not present on my return that air of retrogression and desolation which I might expect if it were left unoccupied and in charge of a caretaker.

My agent assured me that I would have no trouble whatever in letting my place, for it offered many advantages and I expected but a reasonable rent. I desired to leave everything just as it stood, house, furniture, books, horses, cows, and poultry, taking with me only my clothes and personal requisites, and I desired tenants who would come in, bringing only their clothes and personal requisites, which they could quietly take away with them when their lease should expire and I should return home.

In spite, however, of the assurances of the agent it was not easy to let my place. The house was too large for some people; too small for others, and while some applicants had more horses than I had stalls in my

stable, others did not want even the horses I
would leave. I had engaged my steamer
passage, and the day for my departure drew
near and yet no suitable tenants had presented themselves. I had almost come to
the conclusion that the whole matter would
have to be left in the hands of my agent, for
I had no intention whatever of giving up my
projected travels, when early one afternoon
some people came to look at the house.
Fortunately I was at home and I gave myself
the pleasure of personally conducting them
about the premises. It was a pleasure, because as soon as I comprehended the fact
that these applicants desired to rent my
house I wished them to have it.

The family consisted of an elderly gentleman and his wife with a daughter of twenty
or thereabouts. This was a family that suited
me exactly. Three in number, no children,
people of intelligence and position, fond of
the country and anxious for just such a place
as I offered them—what could be better?

The more I walked about and talked with
these good people and showed them my
possessions the more I desired that the
young lady should take my **house**. Of

course, her parents were included in this wish, but it was for her ears that all my remarks were intended, although sometimes addressed to the others, and she was the tenant I labored to obtain. I say labored advisedly, because I racked my brain to think of inducements which might bring them to a speedy and favorable decision.

Apart from the obvious advantages of the arrangement it would be a positive delight to me during my summer wanderings in Europe to think that that beautiful girl would be strolling through my grounds, enjoying my flowers and sitting with her book in the shady nooks I had made so pleasant, lying in my hammocks, spending her evening hours in my study reading my books, writing at my desk and perhaps musing in my easy-chair. Before these applicants appeared it had sometimes pained me to imagine strangers in my home, but no such thought crossed my mind in regard to this young lady, who, if charming in the house and on the lawn, grew positively entrancing when she saw my Jersey cows and my two horses, regarding them with an admiration which even surpassed my own.

I GAVE MYSELF THE PLEASURE OF PERSONALLY CONDUCTING THEM ABOUT

Long before we had completed the tour of inspection I had made up my mind that this young lady should come to live in my house. If obstacles should show themselves they should be removed. I would tear down, I would build, I would paper and paint, I would put in all sorts of electric bells; I would reduce the rent until it suited their notions exactly; I would have my horses' tails banged if she liked that kind of tails better than long ones; I would do anything to make them definitely decide to take the place before they left me. I trembled to think of her going elsewhere and giving other householders a chance to tempt her. She had looked at a good many country houses, but it was quite plain that none of them had pleased her so well as mine.

I left them in my library to talk the matter over by themselves, and in less than ten minutes the young lady herself came out on the lawn to tell me that her father and mother had decided to take the place and would like to speak with me.

"I am so glad," she said as we went in; "I am sure I shall enjoy every hour of our stay here. It is so different from anything we have yet seen."

When everything had been settled I wanted
to take them again over the place and point
out a lot of things I had omitted. I particularly wanted to show them some lovely walks
in the woods, but there was no time, for they
had to catch a train.

Her name was Vincent—Cora Vincent, as
I discovered from her mother's remarks.

As soon as they departed I had my mare
saddled and rode into town to see my agent.
I went into his office exultant.

"I've let my house," I said, "and I want
you to make out the lease and have everything fixed and settled as soon as possible.
This is the address of my tenants."

The agent asked me a good many questions, being particularly anxious to know
what rent had been agreed upon.

"Heavens!" he exclaimed, when I mentioned the sum, "that is ever so much less
than what I told you you could get. I am
in communication now with a party whom I
know would pay you considerably more than
these people. Have you definitely settled
with them? Perhaps it is not too late to
withdraw."

"Withdraw!" I cried. "Never! They

are the only tenants I want. I was determined to get them and I think I must have
lowered the rent four or five times in the
course of the afternoon. I took a big slice
out of it before I mentioned the sum at all.
You see," said I, very impressively, "these
Vincents exactly suit me," and then I went
on to state fully the advantages of the arrangement, omitting, however, any references
to my visions of Miss Vincent swinging in
my hammocks or musing in my study-chair.

It was now May 15th and my steamer
would sail on the 21st. The intervening
days I employed, not in preparing for my
travels, but in making every possible arrangement for the comfort and convenience of my
incoming tenants. The Vincents did not
wish to take possession until June 1st, and I
was sorry they had not applied before I had
engaged my passage, for in that case I would
have selected a later date. A very good
steamer sailed on June 3d and it would have
suited me just as well.

Happening to be in New York one day I
went to the Vincents' city residence to consult with them in regard to some awnings
which I proposed putting up at the back of

the house.   I found no one at home but the
old gentleman, and it made no difference
to him whether the awnings were black and
brown or red and yellow.   I cordially invited him to come out before I left and bring
his family that they might look about the
place to see if there was anything they would
like to have done which had not already been
attended to.   It was so much better, I told
him, to talk over these matters personally
with the owner than with an agent in his absence.   Agents were often very unwilling to
make changes.   Mr. Vincent was a very quiet
and exceedingly pleasant elderly gentleman,
and thanked me very much for my invitation,
but said he did not see how he could find the
time to get out to my house before I sailed.
I did not like to say that it was not at all
necessary for him to neglect his affairs in order to accompany his family to my place,
but I assured him that if any of them wished
to go out at any time before they took possession they must feel at perfect liberty to
do so.

I mentioned this matter to my agent, sug-
gesting that if he happened to be in New
York he might call on the Vincents and re-

peat my invitation. It was not likely that the old gentleman would remember to mention it to his wife and daughter, and it was really important that everything should be made satisfactory before I left.

"It seems to me," he said, smiling a little grimly, "that the Vincents had better be kept away from your house until you have gone. If you do anything more to it you may find out that it would have been more profitable to have shut it up while you are away."

He did call, however, partly because I wished him to and partly because he was curious to see the people I was so anxious to install in my home, and to whom he was to be my legal representative. He reported the next day that he had found no one at home but Miss Vincent, and that she had said that she and her mother would be very glad to come out the next week and go over the place before they took possession.

"Next week!" I exclaimed, "I shall be gone then!"

"But I shall be here," said Mr. Barker "and I'll show them about and take their suggestions."

This did not suit me at all. It annoyed me very much to think of Barker showing Miss Vincent about my place. He was a good looking young man and not at all backward in his manners.

"After all," said I, "I suppose that everything that ought to be done has been done. I hope you told her that."

"Of course not," said he: "that would have been running dead against your orders. Besides, it's my business to show people about places. I don t mind it."

This gave me an unpleasant and uneasy feeling. I wondered if Mr. Barker were the agent I ought to have, and if a middle-aged man with a family and more experience might not be better able to manage my affairs.

"Barker," said I, a little later, "there will be no use of your going every month to the Vincents to collect their rent. I shall write to Mr. Vincent to pay as he pleases. He can send a check monthly or at the end of the season, as it may be convenient. He is perfectly responsible and I would much prefer to have the money in a lump when I come back."

Barker grinned. "All right," said he, "but that's not the way to do business, you know."

I may have been mistaken but I fancied that I saw in my agent's face an expression which indicated that he intended to call on the first day of each month on the pretext of telling Vincent that it was not necessary to pay the rent at any particular time, and that he also proposed to make many other intervening visits to inquire if repairs were needed. This might have been a good deal to get out of his expression but I think I could have got more if I had thought longer.

On the day before that on which I was to sail, my mind was in such a disturbed condition that I could not attend to my packing or anything else. It almost enraged me to think that I was deliberately leaving the country ten days before my tenants would come to my house. There was no reason why I should do this; there were many reasons why I should not; there was Barker. I was now of the opinion that he would personally superintend the removal of the Vincents and their establishment to my home. I remembered that the only sugges-

tion he had made about the improvement of
the place had been the construction of a tennis-court. I knew that he was a champion
player. Confound it! What a dreadful mistake I had made in selecting such a man for
my house agent. With my mind's eye I
could already see Miss Vincent and Barker
selecting a spot for tennis and planning the
arrangements of the court.

I took the first train to New York and went
directly to the steamboat office. It is astonishing how many obstacles can be removed
from a man's path if he will make up his
mind to give them a good kick. I found that
my steamer was crowded. The applications
for passage exceeded the accommodations,
and the agent was delighted to transfer me to
the steamer that sailed on June 3d. I went
home exultant. Barker drove over in the
evening to take his last instructions, and a
blank look came over his face when I told
him that business had delayed my departure
and that I should not sail the next day. If I
had told him that part of that business was
the laying out of a tennis-court he might have
looked blanker.

Of course the date of my departure did not

concern the Vincents, provided the house was vacated by June 1, and I did not inform them of the changes in my plans, but when the mother and daughter came out the next week they were much surprised to find me waiting to receive them instead of Barker. I hope that they were also pleased, and I am sure that they had every reason to be so. Mrs. Vincent, having discovered that I was a most complacent landlord, accommodated herself easily to my disposition and made a number of minor requirements, all of which I granted without the slightest hesitation. I was de-lighted at last to put her into the charge of my housekeeper, and when the two had be-taken themselves to the bed-rooms I invited Miss Vincent to come out with me to select a spot for a tennis-court. The invitation was accepted with alacrity, for tennis, she declared, was a passion with her.

The selection of that tennis-court took nearly an hour, for there were several good places for one and it was hard to make a se-lection, besides I could not lose the opportu-nity of taking Miss Vincent into the woods and showing her the walks I had made and the rustic seats I had placed in pleasant nooks. Of course she would have discovered these, but it was a great deal better for her to know all about them before she came. At last Mrs. Vincent sent a maid to tell her daughter that it was time to go for the train, and the court had not been definitely planned.

The next day I went to Miss Vincent's house with a plan of the grounds, and she and I talked over it until the matter was settled. It was necessary to be prompt about this, as I explained, as there would be a great deal of leveling and rolling to be done.

I also had a talk with the old gentleman about books. There were several large boxes of my books in New York which I had never sent out to my country house. Many of these I thought might be interesting to him, and I offered to have them taken out and left at his disposal. When he heard the titles of some of the books in the collection he was much interested, but insisted that before he made use of them they should be catalogued, as were the rest of my effects. I hesitated a moment, wondering if I could induce Barker to come to New York and catalogue four big boxes of books, when, to my surprise, Miss

Vincent incidentally remarked that if they were in any place where she could get at them she would be pleased to help catalogue them; that sort of thing was a great pleasure to her. Instantly I proposed that I should send the books to the Vincent house; that they should there be taken out so that Mr. Vincent could select those he might care to read during the summer; that I would make a list of these, and if Miss Vincent would assist me I would be grateful for the kindness, and those that were not desired could be returned to the store-house.

What a grand idea was this! I had been internally groaning because I could think of no possible pretence for further interviews with Miss Vincent, and here was something better than I could have imagined. Her father declared that he could not put me to so much trouble, but I would listen to none of his words, and the next morning my books were spread over his library floor.

The selection and cataloguing of the volumes desired occupied the mornings of three days. The old gentleman's part was soon done, but there were many things in the books which were far more interesting to me than their titles, and to which I desired to draw Miss Vincent's attention. All this greatly protracted our labors. She was not only a beautiful girl, but her intelligence and intellectual grasp were wonderful. I could not help telling her what a great pleasure it would be to me to think, while wandering in foreign lands, that such an appreciative family would be enjoying my books and my place.

"You are so fond of your house and everything you have," said she, "that we shall almost feel as if we were depriving you of your rights. But I suppose that Italian lakes and the Alps will make you forget for a time even your beautiful home."

"Not if you are in it," I longed to say, but I restrained myself. I did not believe that it were possible for me to be more in love with that girl than I was at that moment, but, of course, it would be the rankest stupidity to tell her so. To her I was simply her father's landlord.

I went to that house the next day to see that the boxes were properly repacked, and I actually went the next day to see if the right boxes had gone into the country, and the others back to the storehouse. The first day

I saw only the father. The second day it was the mother who assured me that everything had been properly attended to. I began to feel that if I did not wish a decided rebuff I would better not make any more pretences of business at the Vincent house.

There were affairs of my own which should have been attended to and I ought to have gone home and attended to them, but I could not bear to do so. There was no reason to suppose she would go out there before the first of June.

Thinking over the matter many times I came to the conclusion that if I could see her once more I would be satisfied. Then I would go away and carry her image with me into every art gallery, over every glacier and under every lovely sky that I should enjoy abroad, hoping all the time that, taking my place, as it were, in my home, and making my possessions, in a measure, her own, she would indirectly become so well acquainted with me that when I returned I might speak to her without shocking her.

To obtain this final interview there was but one way. I had left my house on Saturday, the Vincents would come on the following Monday and I would sail on Wednesday. I would go on Tuesday to inquire if they found everything to their satisfaction. This would be a very proper attention from a landlord about to leave the country.

When I reached Boynton I determined to walk to my house, for I did not wish to encumber myself with a hired vehicle. I might be asked to stay to luncheon. A very strange feeling came over me as I entered my grounds. They were not mine. For the time being they belonged to somebody else. I was merely a visitor or a trespasser if the Vincents thought proper so to consider me. If they did not like people to walk on the grass I had no right to do it.

None of my servants had been left on the place, and the maid who came to the door informed me that Mr. Vincent had gone to New York that morning and that Mrs. Vincent and her daughter were out driving. I ventured to ask if she thought they would soon return, and she answered that she did not think they would, as they had gone to Rock Lake which, from the way they talked about it, must be a long way off.

Rock Lake! When I had driven over there with my friends we had taken luncheon at the inn and returned in the afternoon. And what did they know of Rock Lake? Who had told them of it? That officious Barker, of course.

"Will you leave a message, sir?" said the maid, who, of course, did not know me.

"No," said I, and as I still stood gazing at the piazza floor she remarked that if I wished to call again she would go out and speak to the coachman and ask him if anything had been said to him about the time of the party's return.

Worse and worse! Their coachman had not driven them! Some one who knew the country had been their companion. They were not acquainted in the neighborhood and there could not be a shadow of a doubt that it was that obtrusive Barker who had indecently thrust himself upon them on the very next day after their arrival, and had thus snatched from me that last interview upon which I had counted so earnestly.

I had no right to ask any more questions; I left no message nor any name, and I had no excuse for saying I would call again.

I got back to my hotel without having met any one whom I knew, and that night I received a note from Barker, stating that he had fully intended coming to the steamer to see me off, but that an engagement would prevent him. He sent, however, his best good wishes for my safe passage and assured me that he would keep me fully informed of the state of my affairs on this side.

"Engagement!" I exclaimed. "Is he going to drive with her again to-morrow?"

My steamer sailed at two o'clock the next day, and after an early breakfast I went to the company's office to see if I could dispose of my ticket. It had become impossible, I told the agent, for me to leave America at present. He said it was a very late hour to sell my ticket, but that he would do what he could, and if an applicant turned up he would give him my room and refund the money. He wanted me to change to another date but I declined to do this. I was not able to say when I should sail.

I now had no plan of action. All I knew was that I could not leave America without finding out something definite about this Barker business. That is to say, if it should

AT THE STEAMSHIP OFFICE.

be complained to me that instead of attending to my business, sending a carpenter to make repairs, if such were necessary, or going personally to the plumber to make sure that that erratic personage would give his attention to any pipes in regard to which Mr. Vincent might have written, Barker should mingle in sociable relations with my tenants and drive or play tennis with the young lady of the house, then would I immediately have done with him. I would withdraw my business from his hands and place it in those of old Mr. Poindexter. More than that, it might be my duty to warn Miss Vincent's parents against Barker. I did not doubt that he was a very good house and land agent, but in selecting him as such I had no idea of introducing him to the Vincents in a social way. In fact, the more I thought about it the more I became convinced that if ever I mentioned Barker to my tenants it would be to warn them against him. From certain points of view he was actually a dangerous man.

This, however, I would not do until I found my agent was really culpable. To discover what Barker had done, what he was doing and what he intended to do, was now my only business in life. Until I had satisfied myself on these points I could not think of starting out upon my travels.

Now that I had determined that I would not start for Europe until I had satisfied myself that Mr. Barker was contenting himself with attending to my business, and not endeavoring to force himself into social relations with my tenants, I was anxious that the postponement of my journey should be unknown to my friends and acquaintances, and I was, therefore, very glad to see in a newspaper, published on the afternoon of the day of my intended departure, my name among the list of passengers who had sailed upon the Mnemonic. For the first time I commended the super-enterprise of a reporter who gave more attention to the timeliness of his news than to its accuracy.

I was stopping at a New York hotel, but I did not wish to stay there. Until I felt myself ready to start on my travels the neighborhood of Boynton would suit me better than anywhere else. I did not wish to go to the town itself, for Barker lived there and I knew many of the townspeople, but there were farm-houses, not far away, where I might spend a week. After considering the matter I thought of something that might suit me. About three miles from my house, on an unfrequented road, was a mill which stood at the end of an extensive sheet of water, in reality a mill pond, but commonly called a lake. The miller, an old man, had recently died, and his house near by was occupied by a newcomer whom I had never seen. If I could get accommodations there it would suit me exactly. I left the train two stations below Boynton and walked over to the mill.

The country-folk in my neighborhood are always pleased to take summer boarders if they can get them, and the miller and his wife were glad to give me a room, not imagining that I was the owner of a good house not far away. The place suited my requirements very well. It was near her and I might live here for a time unnoticed, but what I was going to do with my opportunity I did not know. Several times the conviction forced itself upon me that I should get up at once and go to Europe by the first steamer, and so show myself that I was a man of sense.

This conviction was banished on the second afternoon of my stay at the mill. I was sitting under a tree in the orchard near the house, thinking and smoking my pipe, when along the road which ran by the side of the lake, came Mr. Vincent on my black horse General and his daughter on my mare Sappho. Instinctively I pulled my straw hat over my eyes, but this precaution was not necessary. They were looking at the beautiful lake with its hills and overhanging trees, and saw me not!

When the very tip of Sappho's tail had melted into the foliage of the road I arose to my feet and took a deep breath of the happy air. I had seen her and it was with her father she was riding.

I do not believe I slept a minute that night through thinking of her and feeling glad that I was near her, and that she had been riding with her father.

When the early dawn began to break an idea brighter than the dawn broke upon me: I would get up and go nearer to her. It is amazing how much we lose by not getting up early on the long summer days. How beautiful the morning might be on this earth I never knew until I found myself wandering by the edge of my woods and over my lawn with the tender gray-blue sky above me and all the freshness of the grass and flowers and trees about me, the birds singing among the branches and she sleeping sweetly somewhere within that house with its softly-defined lights and shadows. How I wished I knew what room she occupied!

The beauties and joys of that hour were lost to every person on the place, who were all, no doubt, in their soundest sleep. I did not even see a dog. Quietly and stealthily stepping from bush to hedge I went around the house, and as I drew near the barn I fancied I could hear from a little room adjoining it the snores of the coachman. The lazy rascal would probably not awaken for two or three hours yet, but I would run no risks and in half an hour I had sped away.

Now I knew exactly why I was staying at the house of the miller. I was doing so in order that I might go early in the mornings to my own home, in which the girl I loved lay dreaming, and that for the rest of the day and much of the night I might think of her.

"What place in Europe," I said to myself,

"could be so beautiful, so charming, and so helpful to reflection as this sequestered lake, these noble trees, these stretches of undulating meadow?"

Even if I should care to go abroad, a month or two later would answer all my purposes. Why had I ever thought of spending five months away?

There was a pretty stream which ran from the lake and wended its way through a green and shaded valley, and here with a rod I wandered and fished and thought. The miller had boats, and in one of these I rowed far up the lake where it narrowed into a creek, and between the high hills which shut me out from the world I would float and think.

Every morning, soon after break of day, I went to my home and wandered about my grounds. If it rained I did not mind that; I like a summer rain.

Day by day I grew bolder. Nobody in that household thought of getting up until seven o'clock. For two hours, at least, I could ramble undisturbed through my grounds, and much as I had once enjoyed these grounds, they never afforded me the pleasure they gave me now. In these happy mornings I felt all the life and spirits of a boy. I went into my little field and stroked the sleek sides of my cows as they nibbled the dewy grass. I even peeped through the barred window of Sappho's box, and fed her, as I had been used to doing, with bunches of clover. I saw that the young chickens were flourishing. I went into the garden and noted the growth of the vegetables, feeling glad that she would have so many fine strawberries and tender peas.

I had not the slightest doubt that she was fond of flowers, and for her sake now, as I used to do for my own sake, I visited the flower beds and borders. Not far from the house there was a cluster of old-fashioned pinks which I was sure were not doing very well. They had been there too long, perhaps, and they looked stunted and weak. In the miller's garden I had noticed great beds of these pinks and I asked his wife if I might have some, and she, considering them as mere wild flowers, said I might have as many as I liked. She might have thought I wanted simply the blossoms, but the next morning I went over to my house with a bas-

ket filled with great matted masses of the
plants taken up with the roots and plenty of
earth around them, and after twenty minutes'
work in my own bed of pinks, I had taken
out all the old plants and filled their places
with fresh, luxuriant masses of buds and
leaves and blossoms. How glad she would
be when she saw the fresh life that had come
to that flower bed! With light footsteps I
went away, not feeling the weight of the basket filled with the old plants and roots.

The summer grew and strengthened and
the sun rose earlier, but as that had no effect
upon the rising of the present inhabitants of
my place, it gave me more time for my morning pursuits. Gradually I constituted myself
the regular flower-gardener of the premises.
How delightful the work was, and how foolish I thought I had been never to think of
doing this thing for myself, but no doubt it
was because I was doing it for her that I found
it so pleasant.

Once again I had seen Miss Vincent. It
was in the afternoon and I had rowed myself
to the upper part of the lake, where, with the
high hills and the trees on each side of me, I
felt as if I were alone in the world. Floating

idly along, with my thoughts about three miles away, I heard the sound of oars, and looking out on the open part of the lake I saw a boat approaching. The miller was rowing and in the stern sat an elderly gentleman and a young lady. I knew them in an instant; they were Mr. and Miss Vincent.

With a few vigorous strokes I shot myself into the shadows and rowed up the stream into the narrow stretches among the lily pads, under a bridge and around a little wooded point, where I ran the boat ashore and sprang upon the grassy bank. I did not believe the miller would bring them as far as this, but I went up to a higher spot and watched for half an hour, but I did not see them again. How relieved I was, for it would have been terribly embarrassing had they discovered me, and how disappointed I was that the miller turned back so soon!

I now extended the supervision of my grounds. I walked through the woods, and saw how beautiful they were in the early dawn. I threw aside the fallen twigs and cut away encroaching saplings, which were beginning to encumber the paths I had made, and if I found a bough which hung too low I cut it off. There was a great beech tree, between which and a dogwood I had the year before suspended a hammock. In passing this one morning I was amazed to see a hammock swinging from the hooks I had put in the two trees. This was a retreat which I had supposed no one else would fancy or even think of! In the hammock was a fan, a common Japanese fan. For fifteen minutes I stood looking at that hammock, every nerve a-tingle. Then I glanced around; the spot had been almost unfrequented since last summer; little bushes, weeds and vines had sprung up here and there between the two trees. There were dead twigs and limbs lying about, and the short path to the main walk was much overgrown.

I looked at my watch. It was a quarter to six. I had yet a good hour for work, and with nothing but my pocket-knife and my hands I began to clear away the space about that hammock. When I left it it looked as it used to look when it was my pleasure to lie there and swing and read and reflect.

To approach this spot it was not necessary to go through my grounds, for my bit of woods adjoined a considerable stretch of forest land, and in my morning walks from the mill I often used a path through these woods. The next morning when I took this path I was late because I had unfortunately overslept myself. When I reached the hammock it wanted fifteen minutes to seven o'clock. It was too late for me to do anything, but I was glad to be able to stay there even for a few minutes, to breathe that air, to stand on that ground, to touch that hammock. I did more than that; why shouldn't I? I got into it. It was a better one than that I had hung there; it was delightfully comfortable. At this moment, gently swinging in that woodland solitude, with the sweet odors of the morning all about me, I felt myself nearer to her than I had ever been before.

But I knew I must not revel in this place too long. I was on the point of rising to leave when I heard approaching footsteps. My breath stopped; was I at last to be discovered? This was what came of my reckless security. But perhaps the person, some workman most likely, would pass without noticing me. To remain quiet seemed the best course, and I lay motionless.

But the person approaching turned into

the little pathway; the footsteps came
nearer. I sprang from the hammock. Before me was Miss Vincent!

What was my aspect I know not, but I
have no doubt I turned fiery red. She
stopped suddenly, but she did not turn red.

"Oh, Mr. Ripley," she exclaimed, "good-
morning. You must excuse me. I did not
know——"

That she should have had sufficient self-
possession to say good-morning amazed me.
Her whole appearance, in fact, amazed me.
There seemed to be something wanting in her
manner. I endeavored to get myself into
condition.

"You must be surprised," I said, "to see
me here. You supposed I was in Europe,
but——"

As I spoke I made a couple of steps toward
her, but suddenly stopped. One of my coat
buttons had caught in the meshes of the
hammock. It was confoundedly awkward;
I tried to loosen the button, but it was badly
entangled; then I desperately pulled at it to
tear it off.

"Oh, don't do that," she said. "Let me
unfasten it for you," and taking the threads

of the hammock in one of her little hands and the button in the other she quickly separated them. "I should think buttons would be very inconvenient things, at least, in hammocks," she said smiling; "you see girls don't have any such trouble."

I could not understand her manner; she seemed to take my being there as a matter of course.

"I must beg a thousand pardons for this —this trespass," I said.

"Trespass!" said she with a smile; "people don't trespass on their own land."

"But it is not my land," said I. "It is your father's for the time being. I have no right here whatever. I do not know how to explain, but you must think it very strange to find me here when you supposed I had started for Europe."

"Oh, I knew you had not started for Europe," said she, "because I have seen you working in the grounds."

"Seen me!" I interrupted. "Is it possible?"

"Oh, yes," said she. "I don't know how long you had been coming when I first saw you, but when I found that fresh bed of pinks all transplanted from somewhere, and just as lovely as they could be, instead of the old ones, I spoke to the man, but he did not know anything about it and said he had not had time to do anything to the flowers, whereas I had been giving him credit for ever so much weeding and cleaning up. Then I supposed that Mr. Barker, who is just as kind and attentive as he can be, had done it, but I could hardly believe he was the sort of man to come early in the morning and work out-of-doors "—(oh, how I wish he had come, I thought. If I had caught him here working among the flowers!)—"and when he came that afternoon to play tennis I found that he had been away for two days, and could not have planted the pinks, so I simply got up early one morning and looked out and there I saw you, with your coat off, working just as hard as ever you could."

I stepped back, my mind for a moment a perfect blank.

" What could you have thought of me ? " I exclaimed presently.

" Really, at first I did not know what to think," said she. " Of course, I did not know what had detained you in this country,

but I remembered that I had heard that you
were a very particular person about your
flowers and shrubs and grounds, and that
most likely you thought they would be better
taken care of if you kept an eye on them, and
that when you found there was so much to do
you just went to work and did it. I did not
speak of this to anybody, because if you did
not wish it to be known that you were taking
care of the grounds it was not my business
to tell people about it. But yesterday when
I found this place where I had hung my
hammock so beautifully cleared up and made
so nice and clean and pleasant in every way,
I thought I must come down to tell you how
much obliged I am and also that you ought
not to take so much trouble for us. If you
think the grounds need more attention I will
persuade my father to hire another man, now
and then, to work about the place. Really,
Mr. Ripley, you ought not to have to——"

I was humbled, abashed. She had seen
me at my morning devotions, and this was
the way she interpreted them. She considered me an over-nice fellow who was so
desperately afraid his place would be injured
that he came sneaking around every morning

to see if any damage had been done and to put things to rights.

She stood for a moment as if expecting me to speak, brushed a buzzing fly from her sleeve, and then, looking at me with a gentle smile, she turned a little as if she were about to leave.

I could not let her go without telling her something. Her present opinion of me must not rest in her mind another minute, and yet what story could I devise? How, indeed, could I devise anything with which to deceive a girl who spoke and looked at me as this girl did? I could not do it. I must rush away speechless and never see her again, or I must tell her all. I came a little nearer to her.

"Miss Vincent," said I, "you do not understand at all why I am here, why I have been here so much, why I did not go to Europe. The truth is I could not leave. I do not wish to be away, I want to come here and live here always——"

"Oh, dear," she interrupted, "of course it is natural that you should not want to tear yourself away from your lovely home. It would be very hard for us to go away now,

especially for father and me, for we have
grown to love this place so much, but if you
want us to leave, I dare say——"

"I want you to leave!" I exclaimed.
"Never! When I say that I want to live
here myself, that my heart will not let me go
anywhere else, I mean that I want you to live
here too—you, your mother and father—that
I want——"

"Oh, that would be perfectly splendid,"
she said. "I have ever so often thought that
it was a shame that you should be deprived
of the pleasures you so much enjoy, which I
see you can find here and nowhere else.
Now, I have a plan which I think will work
splendidly. We are a very small family.
Why shouldn't you come here and live with
us? There is plenty of room, and I know
father and mother would be very glad, and
you can pay your board if that would please
you better. You can have the room at the
top of the tower for your study and your
smoking den, and the room under it can be
your bedroom, so you can be just as indepen-
dent as you please of the rest of us, and you
can be living on your own place without interfering with us in the least. In fact, it

would be ever so nice, especially as I am in the habit of going away to the seashore with my aunt every summer for six weeks, and I was thinking how lonely it would be this year for father and mother to stay here all by themselves."

The tower and the room under it! For me! What a contemptibly little-minded and insignificant person she must think me. The words with which I strove to tell her that I wished to live here as lord, with her as my queen, would not come. She looked at me for a moment as I stood on the brink of saying something but not saying it, and then she turned suddenly toward the hammock.

"Did you see anything of a fan I left here?" she said. "I know I left it here, but when I came yesterday it was gone. Perhaps you may have noticed it somewhere."

Now, the morning before, I had taken that fan home with me. It was an awkward thing to carry, but I had concealed it under my coat. It was a contemptible trick, but the fan had her initials on it, and as it was the only thing belonging to her of which I could possess myself, the temptation had been too great to resist. As she stood waiting for my

answer there was a light in her eye which illuminated my perceptions.

" Did you see me take that fan ? " I asked.

" I did," said she.

" Then you know," I exclaimed, stepping
nearer to her, " why it is I did not leave this
country as I intended, why it was impossible
for me to tear myself away from this house,
why it is that I have been here every morning hovering around and doing the things I
have been doing ? "

She looked up at me, and with her eyes she
said, " How could I help knowing ? " She
might have intended to say something with
her lips, but I took my answer from her eyes,
and with a quick impulse of a lover I
stopped her speech.

" You have strange ways," she said, presently, blushing and gently pressing back my
arm ; " I haven't told you a thing."

" Let us tell each other everything now,"
I cried ; and we seated ourselves in the hammock.

It was a quarter of an hour later and we
were still sitting together in the hammock.

" You may think," said she, " that, knowing what I did, it was very queer for me to

come out to you this morning, but I could
not help it. You were getting so dreadfully
careless and were staying so late and doing
things which people would have been bound
to notice, especially as father is always talking about our enjoying the fresh hours of the
morning, that I felt I could not let you go on
any longer. And when it came to that fan
business I saw plainly that you must either
immediately start for Europe, or——"

"Or what," I interrupted.

"Or go to my father and regularly engage
yourself as a——"

I do not know whether she was going to
say gardener or not, but it did not matter; I
stopped her.

It was perhaps twenty minutes later and
we were standing together at the edge of the
woods; she wanted me to come to the house
to take breakfast with them.

"Oh, I could not do that," I said; "they
would be so surprised. I should have so
much to explain before I could even begin to
state my case."

"Well, then explain," said she. "You will
find father on the front piazza. He is always
there before breakfast, and there is plenty of

time. After all that has been said here I cannot go to breakfast and look commonplace while you run away."

"But suppose your father objects?" said I.

"Well, then you will have to go back and take breakfast with your miller," said she.

I never saw a family so little affected by surprises as those Vincents. When I appeared on the front piazza the old gentleman did not jump. He shook hands with me and asked me to sit down, and when I told him everything he did not even ejaculate, but simply folded his hands together and looked out over the railing.

"It seemed strange to Mrs. Vincent and myself," he said, "when we first noticed your extraordinary attachment for our daughter, but after all it was natural enough."

"Noticed it!" I exclaimed; "when did you do that?"

"Very soon," he said. "When you and Cora were cataloguing the books at my house in town I noticed it and spoke to Mrs. Vincent, but she said it was nothing new to her, for it was plain enough on the day when we first met you here that you were letting the

house to Cora, and that she had not spoken
of it to me because she was afraid I might
think it wrong to accept the favorable and
unusual arrangements you were making with
us if I suspected the reason for them. We
talked over the matter, but, of course, we
could do nothing, because there was nothing
to do, and Mrs. Vincent was quite sure you
would write to us from Europe. But when
my man Ambrose told me he had seen some-
one working about the place in the very early
morning, and that as it was a gentleman he
supposed it must be the landlord, for nobody
else would be doing such things, Mrs. Vincent and myself looked out of the window the
next day, and when we found it was indeed you
who were coming here every day we felt that
the matter was serious and were a good deal
troubled. We found, however, that you were
conducting affairs in a very honorable way,
that you were not endeavoring to see Cora,
and that you did not try to have any secret
correspondence with her, and as we had no
right to prevent you from coming on your
grounds, we concluded to remain quiet until
you should take some step which we would
be authorized to notice. Later, when Mr.

Barker came and told me that you had not
gone to Europe and were living with a miller
not far from here——"

" Barker!" I cried. "The scoundrel!"

" You are mistaken, sir," said Mr. Vincent;
" he spoke with the greatest kindness of you,
and said that as it was evident you had your
own reasons for wishing to stay in the neighborhood, and did not wish the fact to be
known, he had spoken of it to no one but me,
and he would not have done this had he not
thought it would prevent embarrassment in
case we should meet."

Would that everlasting Barker ever cease
meddling in my affairs?

"Do you suppose," I asked, "that he
imagined the reason for my staying here?"

"I do not know," said the old gentleman,
"but after the questions I put to him I have
no doubt he suspected it. I made many inquiries of him regarding you, your family,
habits, and disposition, for this was a very
vital matter to me, sir, and I am happy to inform you that he said nothing of you that was
not good, so I urged him to keep the matter
to himself. I determined, however, that if
you continued your morning visits I should

take an early opportunity of accosting you and asking an explanation."

"And you never mentioned anything of this to your daughter?" said I.

"Oh, no," he answered; "we carefully kept everything from her."

"But, my dear sir," said I, rising, "you have given me no answer. You have not told me whether or not you will accept me as a son-in-law."

He smiled. "Truly," he said, "I have not answered you, but the fact is, Mrs. Vincent and I have considered the matter so long, and having come to the conclusion that if you made an honorable and straightforward proposition, and if Cora were willing to accept you, we could see no reason to object to——"

At this moment the front door opened and Cora appeared.

"Are you going to stay to breakfast?" she asked. "Because, if you are, it is ready."

I stayed to breakfast.

I am now living in my own house, not in the two tower rooms, but in the whole mansion, of which my former tenant, Cora, is now mistress supreme. Mr. and Mrs. Vincent ex-

"ARE YOU GOING TO STAY TO BREAKFAST?" SHE ASKED.

pect to spend the next summer here and take care of the house while we are travelling.

Mr. Barker, an excellent fellow and a most thorough business man, still manages my affairs, and there is nothing on the place that flourishes so vigorously as the bed of pinks which I got from the miller's wife.

By the way, when I went back to my lodging on that eventful day, the miller's wife met me at the door.

"I kept your breakfast waiting for you for a good while," said she, "but as you didn't come I supposed you were taking breakfast in your own house and I cleared it away."

"Do you know who I am!" I exclaimed.

"Oh, yes, sir," she said; "we did not at first, but when everybody began to talk about it we couldn't help knowing it."

"Everybody!" I gasped. "And may I ask what you and everybody said about me?"

"I think it was the general opinion, sir," said she, "that you were suspicious of them tenants of yours, and nobody wondered at it, for when city people gets into the country and on other people's property, there's no trusting them out of your sight for a minute."

I could not let the good woman hold this

opinion of my tenants, and I briefly told her the truth. She looked at me with moist admiration in her eyes.

"I am glad to hear that, sir," said she. "I like it very much, but if I was you I wouldn't be in a hurry to tell my husband and the people in the neighborhood about it. They might be a little disappointed at first, for they had a mighty high opinion of you when they thought that you was layin' low here to keep an eye on them tenants of yours."

THE BISHOP'S GHOST AND THE
PRINTER'S BABY

THE BISHOP'S GHOST AND THE PRINTER'S BABY

A ROUND the walls of a certain old church there stood many tombs, and these had been there so long that the plaster with which their lids were fastened down had dried and crumbled so that in most of them there were long cracks under their lids, and out of these the ghosts of the people who had been buried ~~in the tomb~~ were in the habit of escaping at night.

This had been going on for a long time, and, ~~at the period of our story,~~ the tombs were in such bad repair that every night the body of the church was filled with ghosts, so that before daylight one of the sacristans was obliged to come into the church and sprinkle holy water everywhere. This was done to clear the church of ghosts before the first service began, and who does not know that if a ghost is sprinkled with holy water it shrivels

up! This first service was attended almost
exclusively by printers on their way home
from their nightly labors on the journals of
the town.

The tomb which had the largest crack
under its lid belonged to a bishop who had
died more than a hundred years before, and
who had a great reputation for sanctity; so
much so, indeed, that people had been in the
habit of picking little pieces of plaster from
under the lid of his tomb and carrying them
away as holy relics, to prevent disease and
accidents.

This tomb was more imposing than the
others, and stood upon a pedestal, so that the
crack beneath its lid was quite plain to view,
and remarks had been made about having it
repaired.

Very early one morning, before it was time
for the first service, there came into the
church a poor mason, His wife had recently
recovered from a severe sickness, and he was
desirous of making an offering to the church.
But having no money to spare, he had determined that he would repair the bishop's
tomb, and he consequently came to do this
before his regular hours of work began.

All the ghosts were out of their tombs at the time, but they were gathered in the other end of the church, and the mason did not see them, nor did they notice him; and he immediately went to work. He had brought some plaster and a trowel, and it was not long before the crack under the lid of the tomb was entirely filled up, and the plaster made as smooth and neat as when the tomb was new.

When his work was finished, the mason left the church by the little side door which had given him entrance.

Not ten minutes afterward the sacristan came in to sprinkle the church with holy water. Instantly the ghosts began to scatter right and left, and to slip into their tombs as quickly as possible, but when the ghost of the good bishop reached his tomb he found it impossible to get in. He went around and around it, but nowhere could he find the least little chink by which he could enter. The sacristan was walking along the other side of the church, scattering holy water, and in great trepidation the bishop's ghost hastened from tomb to tomb, hoping to find one which was unoccupied, into which he could slip before the

~~sprinkling began on that side of the church.~~
He soon came to ~~one~~ [a tomb] which he thought
might be unoccupied, but he discovered to
his consternation that it was occupied by
the ghost of a young girl who had died of
love.

"Alas! alas!" ~~exclaimed the bishop's
ghost.~~ "How unlucky! Who would have
supposed this to be your tomb?"

"It is not really my tomb," said the ghost
of the young girl. "It is the tomb of Sir
Geoffrey of the Marle, who was killed in battle nigh two centuries ago. I was told that it
~~had been empty for a long time, for~~ his ghost
has gone to Castle Marle, ~~so Not long ago I
came into the church, and finding this tomb~~
unoccupied, I settled here."

"Ah, me!" said the bishop's ghost, "the
sacristan will soon be around here with holy
water. Could not you get out and go to your
own tomb; where is that?"

"Alas, good father," ~~said the ghost of the
young girl,~~ "I have no tomb; I was buried
plainly in the ground, and I do not know that
I could find the place again. But I have no
right to keep you out of this tomb, good
father; it is as much yours as it is mine, so I

will come out and let you enter; ~~truly, you are in great danger~~. As for me, it doesn't matter very much whether I am sprinkled or not."

So the ghost of the young girl slipped out of Sir Geoffrey's tomb, and the bishop's ghost slipped in, ~~but not a minute before the sacristan had reached the place. The ghost of the young girl flitted from one pillar to another until it came near the door, and there it paused, thinking~~ what it should do next. ~~Even if it could find the grave from which it had come, it did not want to go back to such a place; it liked churches~~ better.

Soon the printers began to come in to the early morning service. One of them was very sad, and there were tears in his eyes. He was a young man, not long married, and ~~his child,~~ ✶ baby girl, was so sick that he scarcely expected to find it alive when he should reach home that morning.

The ghost of the young girl was attracted by the sorrowful printer, and when the service was over, and he had left the church, it followed him, keeping itself unseen. The printer found his wife in tears; the poor little baby was very low. It lay upon the bed, its eyes shut, its face pale and pinched, gasping for breath.

~~The mother was obliged to leave the room for a few moments to attend to some household affair, and her husband followed to comfort her, and when they were gone the ghost of the young girl approached the bed and looked down on the little baby. It was nearer death than its parents supposed, and scarcely had they gone before it drew its last breath.~~

The ghost of the young girl bowed its head. It was filled with pity and sympathy for the printer and his wife. In an instant, however, it was seized with an idea, and the next instant it had acted upon it. Scarcely had the spirit of the little baby left its body than the spirit of the young girl entered it.

Now a gentle warmth suffused the form of the little child, a natural color came into its cheeks, it breathed quietly and regularly, and when the printer and his wife came back they found their baby in a healthful sleep. ~~As they stood amazed at the change in the countenance of the child it opened its eyes and smiled upon them.~~

"The crisis is past!" cried the mother.

"She is saved, and it is all because you stopped at the church instead of hurrying home, as you wished to do." The ghost of the young girl knew that this was true, and the baby smiled. ~~again.~~

It was eighteen years later, and the printer's baby had grown into a beautiful young woman. From her early childhood she had been fond of visiting the church, and would spend hours among the tombs reading the inscriptions, and sometimes sitting by ~~them, especially by~~ the tomb of Sir Geoffrey of the Marle. There, when there was nobody by, she used to talk with the bishop's ghost.

~~Late one afternoon she came to the tomb with a happy smile on her face. "Holy father," she said, speaking softly through the crack, "are you not tired of staying so long in this tomb which is not your own?"~~

~~"Truly, I am, daughter," said the bishop's ghost; "but I have no right to complain. I never come back here in the early morning without a feeling of the warmest gratitude to you for having given me a place of refuge.~~ My greatest trouble is caused by the fear that the ghost of Sir Geoffrey ~~of the Marle~~ may some time choose to return. In that case I must give up to him his tomb. And then, where, oh where, shall I go ? "

" Holy father," ~~whispered the girl,~~ " do not trouble yourself ; you shall have your own tomb again, and need fear no one."

" How is that ? " ~~exclaimed the Bishop's ghost. "Tell me quickly, daughter."~~

" This is the way of it," ~~replied the young girl.~~ " When the mason plastered up the crack under the lid of your tomb he seems to have been very careful about the front part of it, but he did not take much pains with the back, where his work was not likely to be seen, so that there the plaster has crumbled and loosened very much, and with a long pin from my hair I have picked out ever so much of it, and now there is a great crack at the back of the tomb, where you can go in and come out ~~just~~ as easily as you ever did. As soon as night shall fall you can leave this tomb and go into your own."

The bishop's ghost could scarcely speak for thankful emotions, and the happy young girl went home to the house of her father, now a prosperous man, and the head printer of the town.

The next evening the young girl went to

the church and hurried to the bishop's tomb.
Therein she found the bishop's ghost, happy
and content.

Sitting on a stone projection at the back of
the tomb, she had a long conversation with
the bishop's ghost, which, in gratitude for
what she had done, gave her all manner of
good advice and counsel. " Above all things,
my dear daughter," said the bishop's ghost,
"do not repeat your first great mistake;
promise me that you will not die of love."

The young girl smiled. "Fear not, good
father," she replied. " When I died of love I
was, in body and soul, but eighteen years old,
and knew no better; now, although my body
is but eighteen, my soul is thirty-six. Fear
not, never again shall I die of love."

CAPTAIN ELI'S BEST EAR

CAPTAIN ELI'S BEST EAR

THE little seaside village of Sponkannis lies so quietly upon a protected spot on our Atlantic coast that it makes no more stir in the world than would a pebble which, held between one's finger and thumb, should be dipped below the surface of a mill-pond and then dropped. About the post-office and the store—both under the same roof—the greater number of the houses cluster, as if they had come for their week's groceries, or were waiting for the mail; while toward the west the dwellings become fewer and fewer, until at last the village blends into a long stretch of sandy coast and scrubby pine-woods. Eastward the village ends abruptly at the foot of a wind-swept bluff, on which no one cares to build.

Among the last houses in the western end of the village stood two neat, substantial dwellings, one belonging to Captain Eli

Bunker, and the other to Captain Cephas
Dyer. These householders were two very re-
spectable retired mariners, the first a wid-
ower about fifty, and the other a bachelor of
perhaps the same age, a few years more or
less making but little difference in this region
of weather-beaten youth and seasoned age.

Each of these good captains lived alone,
and each took entire charge of his own domestic affairs, not because he was poor, but
because it pleased him to do so. When Captain Eli retired from the sea he was the owner of a good vessel, which he sold at a fair
profit; and Captain Cephas had made money
in many a voyage before he built his house in
Sponkannis and settled there.

When Captain Eli's wife was living, she
was his household manager; but Captain
Cephas had never had a woman in his house,
except during the first few months of his
occupancy, when certain female neighbors
came in occasionally to attend to little matters of cleaning which, according to popular
notions, properly belong to the sphere of
woman.

But Captain Cephas soon put an end to
this sort of thing. He did not like a woman's

ways, especially her ways of attending to domestic affairs. He liked to live in sailor fashion, and to keep house in sailor fashion. In his establishment everything was shipshape, and everything which could be stowed away was stowed away, and, if possible, in a bunker. The floors were holystoned nearly every day, and the whole house was repainted about twice a year, a little at a time, when the weather was suitable for this marine recreation. Things not in frequent use were lashed securely to the walls, or perhaps put out of the way by being hauled up to the ceiling by means of blocks and tackle. His cooking was done sailor fashion, like everything else, and he never failed to have plum-duff on Sunday. His well was near his house, and every morning he dropped into it a lead and line, and noted down the depth of water. Three times a day he entered in a little note-book the state of the weather, the height of the mercury in barometer and thermometer, the direction of the wind, and special weather points when necessary.

Captain Eli managed his domestic affairs in an entirely different way. He kept house woman fashion, not, however, in the manner of an ordinary woman, but after the manner of his late wife, Miranda Bunker, now dead some seven years. Like his friend, Captain Cephas, he had had the assistance of his female neighbors during the earlier days of his widowerhood. But he soon found that these women did not do things as Miranda used to do them, and although he frequently suggested that they should endeavor to imitate the methods of his late consort, they did not even try to do things as she used to do them, preferring their own ways. Therefore it was that Captain Eli determined to keep house by himself, and to do it, as nearly as his nature would allow, as Miranda used to do it. He swept his floors and he shook his door-mats, he washed his paint with soap and hot water, and he dusted his furniture with a soft cloth, which he afterward stuck behind a chest of drawers. He made his bed very neatly, turning down the sheet at the top, and setting the pillow upon edge, smoothing it carefully after he had done so. His cooking was based on the methods of the late Miranda; he had never been able to make bread rise properly, but he had always liked ship biscuit, and he now greatly preferred them to the risen bread made by his neighbors ; and as to coffee and the plainer articles of food with which he furnished his table, even Miranda herself would not have objected to them had she been alive and very hungry.

The houses of the two captains were not very far apart, and they were good neighbors, often smoking their pipes together and talking of the sea. But this was always on the little porch in front of Captain Cephas's house, or by his kitchen fire in the winter. Captain Eli did not like the smell of tobacco-smoke in his house, or even in front of it in summer-time, when the doors were open. He had no objection himself to the odor of tobacco, but it was contrary to the principles of woman-housekeeping that rooms should smell of it, and he was always true to those principles.

It was late in a certain December, and through the village there was a pleasant little flutter of Christmas preparations. Captain Eli had been up to the store, and he had stayed there a good while, warming himself by the stove, and watching the women coming in to buy things for Christmas. It was strange how many things they bought for

presents or for holiday use—fancy soap and
candy, handkerchiefs and little woollen shawls
for old people, and a lot of pretty little things
which he knew the use of, but which Captain
Cephas would never have understood at all
had he been there.

As Captain Eli came out of the store he
saw a cart in which were two good-sized
Christmas-trees which had been cut in the
woods, and were going, one to Captain
Holmes's house, and the other to Mother
Nelson's. Captain Holmes had grandchil-
dren, and Mother Nelson, with never a child
of her own, good old soul, had three little
orphan nieces who never wanted for anything needful at Christmas-time, or any other
time.

Captain Eli walked home very slowly,
taking observations in his mind. It was
more than seven years since he had had anything to do with Christmas, except that on
that day he had always made himself a
mince-pie, the construction and the con-
sumption of which were equally difficult. It
is true that neighbors had invited him, and
they had invited Captain Cephas, to their
Christmas dinners, but neither of these

worthy seamen had ever accepted any of these invitations. Even holiday food, when not cooked in sailor fashion, did not agree with Captain Cephas, and it would have pained the good heart of Captain Eli if he had been forced to make believe to enjoy a Christmas dinner so very inferior to those which Miranda used to set before him.

But now the heart of Captain Eli was gently moved by a Christmas flutter. It had been foolish, perhaps, for him to go up to the store at such a time as this, but the mischief had been done. Old feelings had come back to him, and he would be glad to celebrate Christmas this year if he could think of any good way to do it; and the result of his mental observations was that he went over to Captain Cephas's house to talk to him about it.

Captain Cephas was in his kitchen, smoking his third morning pipe. Captain Eli filled his pipe, lighted it, and sat down by the fire.

" Cap'n," said he, " what do you say to our keepin' Christmas this year? A Christmas dinner is no good if it's got to be eat alone, and you and me might eat ourn together. It might be in my house, or it might be in your house; it won't make no great difference to me, which. Of course, I like woman housekeepin', as is laid down in the rules of service for my house; but next best to that I like sailor housekeepin', so I don't mind which house the dinner is in, Cap'n Cephas, so it suits you."

Captain Cephas took his pipe from his mouth. "You're pretty late thinkin' about it," said he, "for day after to-morrow's Christmas."

"That don't make no difference," said Captain Eli. "What things we want that are not in my house or your house we can easily get either up at the store or else in the woods."

"In the woods!" exclaimed Captain Cephas. "What in the name of thunder do you expect to get in the woods for Christmas?"

"A Christmas-tree," said Captain Eli. "I thought it might be a nice thing to have a Christmas-tree for Christmas. Captain Holmes has got one, and Mother Nelson's got another. I guess nearly everybody's got one. It won't cost anything—I can go and cut it."

Captain Cephas grinned a grin, as if a great
leak had been sprung in the side of a vessel,
stretching nearly from stem to stern.

"A Christmas-tree!" he exclaimed. "Well,
I am blessed! But look here, Cap'n Eli; you
don't know what a Christmas-tree's fer; it's
fer children, and not fer grown-ups. Nobody
ever does have a Christmas-tree in any house
where there ain't no children."

Captain Eli rose and stood with his back
to the fire. "I didn't think of that," he said,
"but I guess it's so; and when I come to
think of it, a Christmas isn't much of a
Christmas, anyway, without children."

"You never had none," said Captain Cephas, "and you've kept Christmas."

"Yes," replied Captain Eli, reflectively;
"we did do it, but there was always a lack-
ment—Miranda has said so, and I have said
so."

"You didn't have no Christmas-tree," said
Captain Cephas.

"No, we didn't; but I don't think that
folks was as much set on Christmas-trees
then as they 'pear to be now. I wonder," he
continued, thoughtfully gazing at the ceiling,
"if we was to fix up a Christmas-tree—and

you and me's got a lot of pretty things that
we've picked up all over the world, that would
go miles ahead of anything that could be
bought at the store for Christmas-trees—if
we was to fix up a tree, real nice, if we
couldn't get some child or other that wasn't
likely to have a tree to come in and look at
it, and stay awhile, and make Christmas more
like Christmas; and then when it went away
it could take along the things that was hang-
in' on the tree, and keep 'em for its own."

"That wouldn't work," said Captain Cephas. "If you get a child into this business,
you must let it hang up its stockin' before it
goes to bed, and find it full in the mornin',
and then tell it an all-fired lie about Santa
Claus if it asks any questions. Most children
think more of stockin's than they do of trees;
so I've heard, at least."

"I've got no objections to stockin's," said
Captain Eli. "If it wanted to hang one up,
it could hang one up either here or in my
house, wherever we kept Christmas."

"You couldn't keep a child all night," sar-
donically remarked Captain Cephas, "and no
more could I; for if it was to get up a croup
in the night, it would be as if we was on

a lee shore with anchors draggin' and a gale
a-blowin'.' "

"That's so," said Captain Eli; "you've
put it fair. I suppose if we did keep a child
all night, we'd have to have some sort of a
woman within hail in case of a sudden blow."

Captain Cephas sniffed. "What's the good
of talkin'?" said he. "There ain't no child,
and there ain't no woman that you could hire
to sit all night on my front step or on your
front step a-waitin' to be piped on deck in
case of croup."

"No," said Captain Eli. "I don't suppose
there's any child in this village that ain't
goin' to be provided with a Christmas-tree or
a Christmas-stockin', or perhaps both, except,
now I come to think of it, that little gal that
was brought down here with her mother last
summer, and has been kept by Mrs. Crumley
sence her mother died."

"And won't be kept much longer," said
Captain Cephas; "for I've hearn Mrs. Crumley say she couldn't afford it."

"That's so,' said Captain Eli. "If she
can't afford to keep the little gal, she can't
afford to give no Christmas-trees nor stockin's; and so it seems to me, Cap'n, that that

little gal would be a pretty good child to help us keep Christmas."

"You're all the time forgettin'," said the other, "that nuther of us can keep a child all night."

Captain Eli seated himself, and looked ponderingly into the fire. "You're right, Cap'n," said he; "we'd have to ship some woman to take care of her. Of course, it wouldn't be no use to ask Mrs. Crumley?"

Captain Cephas laughed. "I should say not."

"And there doesn't seem to be anybody else," said his companion. "Can you think of anybody, Cap'n?"

"There ain't anybody to think of," replied Captain Cephas, "unless it might be Eliza Trimmer; she's generally ready enough to do anything that turns up. But she wouldn't be no good—her house is too far away for either you or me to hail her in case a croup came up suddint."

"That's so," said Captain Eli; "she does live a long way off."

"So that settles the whole business," said Captain Cephas. "She's too far away to come if wanted, and nuther of us couldn't

keep no child without somebody to come if
they was wanted, and it's no use to have a
Christmas-tree without a child. A Christmas
without a Christmas-tree don't seem agreeable to you, Cap'n, so I guess we'd better
get along just the same as we've been in the
habit of doin', and eat our Christmas dinner, as we do our other meals, in our own
houses."

Captain Eli looked into the fire. "I don't
like to give up things if I can help it. That
was always my way. If wind and tide's
ag'in' me, I can wait till one or the other, or
both of them, serve."

"Yes," said Captain Cephas; "you was
always that kind of a man."

"That's so. But it does 'pear to me as if
I'd have to give up this time; though it's a
pity to do it, on account of the little gal, for
she ain't likely to have any Christmas this
year. She's a nice little gal, and takes as
natural to navigation as if she'd been born
at sea. I've given her two or three things
because she's so pretty, but there's nothin'
she likes so much as a little ship I gave her."

"Perhaps she was born at sea," remarked
Captain Cephas.

"Perhaps she was," said the other ; "and that makes it the bigger pity."

For a few moments nothing was said. Then Captain Eli suddenly exclaimed, "I'll tell you what we might do, Cap'n ; we might ask Mrs. Trimmer to lend a hand in givin' the little gal a Christmas. She ain't got nobody in her house but herself, and I guess she'd be glad enough to help give that little gal a regular Christmas. She could go and get the child and bring her to your house or to my house, or wherever we're goin' to keep Christmas, and——"

"Well," said Captain Cephas, with an air of scrutinizing inquiry, "what ? "

"Well," replied the other, a little hesitatingly, "so far as I'm concerned—that is, I don't mind one way or the other—she might take her Christmas dinner along with us and the little gal, and then she could fix her stockin' to be hung up, and help with the Christmas tree, and——"

"Well," demanded Captain Cephas, "what ?"

"Well," said Captain Eli, "she could—that is, it doesn't make any difference to me one way or the other—she might stay all night at whatever house we kept Christmas in, and then you and me might spend the night in the other house, and then she could be ready there to help the child in the mornin', when she came to look at her stockin'."

Captain Cephas fixed upon his friend an earnest glare. "That's pretty considerable of an idea to come upon you so suddint," said he; "but I can tell you one thing : there ain't a-goin' to be any such doin's in my house. If you choose to come over here to sleep, and give up your house to any woman you can find to take care of the little gal, all right; but the thing can't be done here."

There was a certain severity in these remarks, but they appeared to affect Captain Eli very pleasantly.

"Well," said he, "if you're satisfied, I am. I'll agree to any plan you choose to make. It doesn't matter to me which house it's in, and if you say my house, I say my house ; all I want is to make the business agreeable to all concerned. Now it's time for me to go to my dinner ; and this afternoon we'd better go and try to get things straightened out, because the little gal, and whatever woman comes with her, ought to be at my house to-morrow before dark. S'posin' we divide up this business : I'll go and see Mrs. Crumley about the little gal, and you can go and see Mrs. Trimmer."

"No, sir," promptly replied Captain Cephas, "I don't go to see no Mrs. Trimmer. You can see both of them just the same as you can see one—they're all along the same way. I'll go cut the Christmas-tree."

"All right," said Captain Eli ; "it don't make no difference to me which does which ; but if I was you, Cap'n, I'd cut a good big tree, because we might as well have a good one while we're about it."

When he had eaten his dinner and washed up his dishes, and had put everything away in neat, housewifely order, Captain Eli went to Mrs. Crumley's house, and very soon finished his business there. Mrs. Crumley kept the only house which might be considered a boarding-house in the village of Sponkannis ; and when she had consented to take charge of the little girl who had been left on her hands she had hoped it would not be very long before she would hear from some of her relatives in regard to her maintenance. But she had heard nothing, and had now ceased to expect to hear anything, and in consequence had frequently remarked that she must dispose of the child some way or other, for she couldn't afford to keep her any longer. Even an absence of a day or two at the house of the good captain would be some relief, and Mrs. Crumley readily consented to the Christmas scheme. As to the little girl, she was delighted. She already looked upon Captain Eli as her best friend in the world.

It was not so easy to go to Mrs. Trimmer's house and put the business before her. "It ought to be plain sailin' enough," Captain Eli said to himself, over and over again; "but for all that it don't seem to be plain sailin'."

But he was not a man to be deterred by difficult navigation, and he walked straight to Eliza Trimmer's house.

Mrs. Trimmer was a comely woman, about thirty-five, who had come to the village a year before, and had maintained herself, or at least, had tried to, by dressmaking and plain sewing. She had lived at Stetford, a seaport about twenty miles away, and from there, three years before, her husband, Captain Trimmer, had sailed away in a good-sized schooner, and had never returned. She had come to Sponkannis because she thought that there she could live cheaper and get more work than in her former home. She had found the first quite possible, but her success in regard to the work had not been very great.

When Captain Eli entered Mrs. Trimmer's little room, he found her busy mending a sail. Here fortune favored him. "You turn your hand to 'most anything, Mrs. Trimmer," said he, after he had greeted her.

"Oh, yes," she answered, with a smile; "I am obliged to do that. Mending sails is pretty heavy work, but it's better than nothing."

"I had a notion," said he, "that you was ready to turn your hand to any good kind of business, so I thought I would step in and ask you if you'd turn your hand to a little bit of business I've got on the stocks."

She stopped sewing on the sail, and listened while Captain Eli laid his plan before her. "It's very kind in you and Captain Cephas to think of all that," said she. "I have often noticed that poor little girl, and pitied her. Certainly I'll come, and you needn't say anything about paying me for it. I wouldn't think of asking to be paid for doing a thing like that. And besides"—she smiled again as she spoke—"if you are going to give me a Christmas dinner, as you say, that will make things more than square."

Captain Eli did not exactly agree with her; but he was in very good humor, and she was in good humor, and the matter was soon settled, and Mrs. Trimmer promised to come to the captain's house in the morning and help about the Christmas-tree, and in the afternoon to go to get the little girl from Mrs. Crumley's and bring her to the house.

Captain Eli was delighted with the arrangements. "Things now seem to be goin' along before a spankin' breeze," said he. "But I don't know about the dinner; I guess you will have to leave that to me. I don't believe Captain Cephas could eat a woman-cooked dinner. He's accustomed to livin' sailor fashion, you know, and he has declared over and over again to me that woman-cookin' doesn't agree with him."

"But I can cook sailor fashion," said Mrs. Trimmer—"just as much sailor fashion as you or Captain Cephas; and if he don't believe it, I'll prove it to him; so you needn't worry about that."

When the Captain had gone, Mrs. Trimmer gayly put away the sail. There was no need to finish it in a hurry, and no knowing when she would get her money for it when it was done. No one had asked her to a Christmas dinner that year, and she had expected to have a lonely time of it; but it would be very pleasant to spend Christmas with the little girl and the two good captains. Instead of sewing any more on the sail, she got out some of her own clothes to see if they needed anything done to them.

The next morning Mrs. Trimmer went to Captain Eli's house, and finding Captain Cephas there, they all set to work at the Christmas-tree, which was a very fine one, and had been planted in a box. Captain Cephas had brought over a bundle of things from his house, and Captain Eli kept running here and there, bringing each time that he returned some new object, wonderful or pretty, which he had brought from China or Japan or Korea, or some spicy island of the Eastern seas, and nearly every time he came with these treasures Mrs. Trimmer declared that these things were too good to put upon a Christmas-tree, even for such a nice little girl as the one for which

CAPTAIN CEPHAS HAD BROUGHT OVER A BUNDLE OF THINGS.

that tree was intended. The presents which Captain Cephas brought were much more suitable for the purpose : they were odd and funny, and some of them pretty, but not expensive, as were the fans and bits of shell-work and carved ivories which Captain Eli wished to tie upon the twigs of the tree.

There was a good deal of talk about all this, but Captain Eli had his own way.

"I don't suppose, after all," said he, "that the little gal ought to have all the things. This is such a big tree that it's more like a family tree. Cap'n Cephas can take some of my things, and I can take some of his things, and, Mrs. Trimmer, if there's anything you like, you can call it your present, and take it for your own ; so that will be fair and comfortable all round. What I want is to make everybody satisfied."

"I'm sure I think they ought to be," said Mrs. Trimmer, looking very kindly at Captain Eli.

Mrs. Trimmer went home to her own house to dinner, and in the afternoon she brought the little girl. She had said there ought to be an early supper, so that the child would have time to enjoy the Christmas-tree before she became sleepy.

This meal was prepared entirely by Captain Eli, and in sailor fashion, not woman fashion, so that Captain Cephas could make no excuse for eating his supper at home. Of course they all ought to be together the whole of that Christmas eve. As for the big dinner on the morrow, that was another affair, for Mrs. Trimmer undertook to make Captain Cephas understand that she had always cooked for Captain Trimmer in sailor fashion, and if he objected to her plum-duff, or if anybody else objected to her mince-pie, she was going to be very much surprised.

Captain Cephas ate his supper with a good relish, and was still eating when the rest had finished. As to the Christmas-tree, it was the most valuable, if not the most beautiful, that had ever been set up in that region. It had no candles upon it, but was lighted by three lamps and a ship's lantern, placed in the four corners of the room, and the little girl was as happy as if the tree were decorated with little dolls and glass balls. Mrs. Trimmer was intensely pleased and interested to see the child so happy, and Captain Eli was much pleased and interested to see the child and Mrs. Trimmer so happy, and Captain Cephas was interested, and perhaps a little amused in a superior fashion, to see Captain Eli and Mrs. Trimmer and the little child so happy.

Then the distribution of the presents began. Captain Eli asked Captain Cephas if he might have the wooden pipe that the latter had brought for his present. Captain Cephas said he might take it, for all he cared, and be welcome to it. Then Captain Eli gave Captain Cephas a red bandanna handkerchief of a very curious pattern, and Captain Cephas thanked him kindly. After which Captain Eli bestowed upon Mrs. Trimmer a most beautiful tortoise-shell comb, carved and cut and polished in a wonderful way, and with it he gave a tortoise-shell fan, carved in the same fashion, because he said the two things seemed to belong to each other and ought to go together; and he would not listen to one word of what Mrs. Trimmer said about the gifts being too good for her, and that she was not likely ever to use them.

"It seems to me," said Captain Cephas,

" that you might be giving something to the little gal."

Then Captain Eli remembered that the child ought not to be forgotten, and her soul was lifted into ecstasy by many gifts, some of which Mrs. Trimmer declared were too good for any child in this wide, wide world ; but Captain Eli answered that they could be taken care of by somebody until the little girl was old enough to know their value.

Then it was discovered that, unbeknown to anybody else, Mrs. Trimmer had put some presents on the tree, which were things which had been brought by Captain Trimmer from somewhere in the far East or the distant West. These she bestowed upon Captain Cephas and Captain Eli, and the end of all this was that in the whole of Sponkannis, from the foot of the bluff to the east, to the very last house on the shore to the west, there was not one Christmas eve party so happy as this one.

Captain Cephas was not quite so happy as the three others were, but he was very much interested. About nine o'clock the party broke up, and the two captains put on their caps and buttoned up their pea-jackets, and started for Captain Cephas's house; but not before Captain Eli had carefully fastened every window and every door except the front door, and had told Mrs. Trimmer how to fasten that when they had gone, and had given her a boatswain's whistle, which she might blow out of the window if there should be a sudden croup, and it should be necessary for anyone to go anywhere. He was sure he could hear it, for the wind was exactly right for him to hear a whistle from his house. When they had gone Mrs. Trimmer put the little girl to bed, and was delighted to find in what a wonderfully neat and womanlike fashion that house was kept.

It was nearly twelve o'clock that night when Captain Eli, sleeping in his bunk opposite that of Captain Cephas, was aroused by hearing a sound. He had been lying with his best ear uppermost, so that he should hear anything if there happened to be anything to hear; and he did hear something, but it was not a boatswain's whistle. It was a prolonged cry, and it seemed to come from the sea.

In a moment Captain Eli was sitting on the side of his bunk, listening intently. **Again** came the cry. The window toward the sea was slightly open, and he heard it plainly.

"Cap'n!" said he, and at the word Captain Cephas was sitting on the side of his bunk, listening. He knew from his companion's attitude, plainly visible in the light of a lantern which hung on a hook at the other end of the room, that he had been awakened to listen. Again came the cry.

"That's distress at sea," said Captain Cephas. "Harken!"

They listened again for nearly a minute, when the cry was repeated.

"Bounce on deck, boys!" said Captain Cephas, getting out on the floor. "There's some one in distress offshore."

Captain Eli jumped to the floor, and began to dress quickly.

"It couldn't be a call from land?" he asked hurriedly; "It don't sound a bit to you like a boatswain's whistle, does it?"

"No," said Captain Cephas, disdainfully. "It's a call from sea." And then, seizing a lantern, he rushed down the companionway.

As soon as he was convinced that it was a call from sea, Captain Eli was one in feeling and action with Captain Cephas. The latter hastily opened the drafts of the kitchen stove, and put on some wood, and by the time this was done Captain Eli had the kettle filled and on the stove. Then they clapped on their caps and their pea-jackets, each took an oar from a corner in the back hall, and together they ran down to the beach.

The night was dark, but not very cold, and Captain Cephas had been to the store that morning in his boat. Whenever he went to the store, and the weather permitted, he rowed there in his boat rather than walk. At the bow of the boat, which was now drawn up on the sand, the two men stood and listened. Again came the cry from the sea.

"It's something ashore on the Turtle-back Shoal," said Captain Cephas.

"Yes," said Captain Eli; "and it's some small craft, for that cry is down pretty nigh to the water."

"Yes," said Captain Cephas; "and there's only one man aboard, or else they'd take turns a-hollerin'."

"He's a stranger," said Captain Eli, "or he wouldn't have tried, even with a catboat, to get in over that shoal on ebb-tide."

As they spoke they ran the boat out into

the water and jumped in, each with an oar.
Then they pulled for the Turtle-back Shoal.

Although these two captains were men of
fifty or thereabout, they were as strong and
tough as any young fellows in the village, and
they pulled with steady strokes, and sent the
heavy boat skimming over the water, not in a
straight line toward the Turtle-back Shoal,
but now a few points in the darkness this
way, and now a few points in the darkness
that way, then with a great curve to the south
through the dark night, keeping always near
the middle of the only good channel out of
the bay when the tide was ebbing.

Now the cries from seaward had ceased,
but the two captains were not discouraged.

"He's heard the thumpin' of our oars,"
said Captain Cephas.

"He's listenin', and he'll sing out again if
he thinks we're goin' wrong," said Captain
Eli ; "of course he don't know anything about
that."

And so when they made the sweep to the
south the cry came again, and Captain Eli
grinned. "We needn't to spend no breath
hollerin'," said he ; "he'll hear us makin' for
him in a minute."

When they came to head for the Shoal they lay on their oars for a moment while Captain Cephas turned the lantern in the bow, so that its light shone out ahead. He had not wanted the shipwrecked person to see the light when it would seem as if the boat were rowing away from him. He had heard of castaway people who would get so wild when they imagined that a ship or boat was going away from them that they would jump overboard.

When the two captains reached the shoal, they found there a catboat aground, with one man aboard. His tale was quickly told. He had expected to run into the little bay that afternoon, but the wind had fallen, and in trying to get in after dark, and being a stranger, he had run aground. If he had not been so cold, he said, he would have been willing to stay there till the tide rose ; but he was getting chilled, and seeing a light not far away, he concluded to call for help as long as his voice held out.

The two captains did not ask many questions. They helped anchor the catboat, and then they took the man on their boat and rowed him to shore. He was getting chilled sitting out there doing nothing, and so when they reached the house they made him some hot grog, and promised in the morning, when the tide rose, they would go out and help him bring his boat in. Then Captain Cephas showed the stranger to a bunk, and they all went to bed. Such experiences had not enough of novelty to the good captains to keep them awake five minutes.

In the morning they were all up very early, and the stranger, who proved to be a seafaring man with bright blue eyes, said that, as his catboat seemed to be riding all right at its anchorage, he did not care to go out after her just yet. Any time during flood-tide would do for him, and he had some business that he wanted to attend to as soon as possible.

This suited the two captains very well, for they wished to be on hand when the little girl discovered her stocking.

"Can you tell me," said the stranger, as he put on his cap, "where I can find a Mrs. Trimmer, who lives in this village?"

At these words all the sturdy stiffness which, from his youth up, had characterized the legs of Captain Eli entirely went out of them, and he sat suddenly upon a bench.

For a few moments there was silence; then Captain Cephas, who thought some answer should be made to the question, nodded his head.

"I want to see her as soon I as can," said the stranger. "I have come to see her on particular business that will be a surprise to her. I wanted to be here before Christmas began, and that's the reason I took that cat-boat from Stetford, because I thought I'd come quicker that way than by land. But the wind fell, as I told you. If either one of you would be good enough to pilot me to where Mrs. Trimmer lives, or to any point where I can get a sight of the place, I'd be obliged."

Captain Eli rose, and with hurried but unsteady steps went into the house (for they had been upon the little piazza), and beckoned to his friend to follow. The two men stood in the kitchen and looked at each other. The face of Captain Eli was of the hue of a clam-shell.

"Go with him, Cap'n," he said in a hoarse whisper; "I can't do it."

"To your house?" inquired the other.

"Of course; take him to my house. There

ain't no other place where she is. Take him
along."

Captain Cephas's countenance wore an air
of the deepest concern, but he thought that
the best thing to do was to get the stranger
away.

As they walked rapidly toward Captain
Eli's house there was very little said by
either Captain Cephas or the stranger. The
latter seemed anxious to give Mrs. Trimmer
a surprise, and not to say anything which
might enable another person to interfere with
his project.

The two men had scarcely stepped upon
the piazza when Mrs. Trimmer, who had been
expecting early visitors, opened the door.
She was about to call out "Merry Christmas!"
but, her eyes falling upon a stranger, the
words stopped at her lips. First she turned
red, then she turned pale, and Captain Cephas thought she was about to fall ; but before she could do this the stranger had her
in his arms. She opened her eyes, which for
a moment she had closed, and gazing into his
face, she put her arms around his neck.
Then Captain Cephas came away, without
thinking of the little girl and the pleasure

she would have in discovering her Christmas stocking.

When he had been left alone, Captain Eli sat down near the kitchen stove, close to the very kettle which he had filled with water to heat for the benefit of the man he had helped bring in from the sea, and, with his elbows on his knees and his fingers in his hair, he darkly pondered.

"If I'd only slept with my hard-o'-hearin' ear up," he said to himself, "I'd never have heard it."

In a few moments his better nature condemned this thought.

"That's next to murder," he muttered; "for he couldn't have kept himself from fallin' asleep out there in the cold and when the tide riz he'd have been blowed out to sea with this wind. If I hadn't heard him, Captain Cephas never would, for he wasn't primed up to wake, as I was."

But, notwithstanding his better nature, Captain Eli was again saying to himself, when his friend returned, "If I'd only slept with my other ear up!"

Like the honest, straightforward mariner he was, Captain Cephas made an exact report of the facts. "They was huggin' when I left them," he said, "and I expect they went indoors pretty soon, for it was too cold outside. It 's an all-fired shame she happened to be in your house, Cap'n; that's all I've got to say about it. It 's a thunderin' shame."

Captain Eli made no answer. He still sat with his elbows on his knees and his hands in his hair.

"A better course than you laid down for these Christmas times was never dotted on a chart," continued Captain Cephas. "From port of sailin' to port of entry you laid it down clear and fine; but it seems there was rocks that wasn't marked on the chart."

"Yes," groaned Captain Eli; "there was rocks."

Captain Cephas made no attempt to comfort his friend, but went to work to get breakfast.

When that meal — a rather silent one — was over, Captain Eli felt better. "There was rocks," he said, "and not a breaker to show where they lay, and I struck 'em bow on. So that's the end of that voyage; but I've tuk to my boats, Cap'n, I've tuk to my boats."

"I'm glad to hear you've tuk to your boats," said Captain Cephas, with an approving glance upon his friend.

About ten minutes afterward Captain Eli said, "I'm goin' up to my house."

"By yourself?" said the other.

"Yes, by myself; I'd rather go alone. I don't intend to mind anything, and I'm goin' to tell her that she can stay there and spend Christmas,— the place she lives in ain't no place to spend Christmas,—and she can make the little gal have a good time, and go 'long just as we intended to go 'long — plum-duff and mince-pie all the same; and I can stay here, and you and me can have our Christmas dinner together, if we choose to give it that name. And if she ain't ready to go to-morrow, she can stay a day or two longer; it's all the same to me, if it's the same to you, Cap'n."

And Captain Cephas having said that it was the same to him, Captain Eli put on his cap and buttoned up his pea-jacket, declaring that the sooner he got to his house the better, as she might be thinking that she would have to move out of it now that things were different.

Before Captain Eli reached his house he saw something which pleased him. He saw the sea-going stranger, with his back toward him, walking rapidly in the direction of the village store.

Captain Eli quickly entered his house, and in the doorway of the room where the tree was he met Mrs. Trimmer, beaming brighter than any morning sun that ever rose.

"Merry Christmas!" she exclaimed, holding out both her hands. "I've been wondering and wondering when you'd come to bid me 'Merry Christmas'—the merriest Christmas I've ever had."

Captain Eli took her hands and bid her "Merry Christmas" very gravely. She looked a little surprised. "What's the matter, Captain Eli?" she exclaimed. "You don't seem to say that as if you meant it."

"Oh, yes, I do," he answered; "this must be an all-fired—I mean a thunderin' happy Christmas for you, Mrs. Trimmer."

"Yes," said she, her face beaming again. "And to think that it should happen on Christmas-day—that this blessed morning, before anything else happened, my Bob, my only brother, should——"

"Your what!" roared Captain Eli, as if he had been shouting orders in a raging storm.

Mrs. Trimmer stepped back almost frightened. "My brother," said she. "Didn't he tell you he was my brother — my brother Bob, who sailed away a year before I was married, and who has been in Africa and China and I don't know where? It's so long since I heard that he'd gone into trading at Singapore that I'd given him up as married and settled in foreign parts; and here he has come to me as if he'd tumbled from the sky on this blessed Christmas morning."

Captain Eli made a step forward, his face very much flushed.

"Your brother, Mrs. Trimmer — did you really say it was your brother?"

"Of course it is," said she. "Who else could it be?" Then she paused for a moment and looked steadfastly at the captain.

"You don't mean to say, Captain Eli," she asked, "that you thought it was——"

"Yes, I did," said Captain Eli, promptly.

Mrs. Trimmer looked straight in the captain's eyes, then she looked on the ground. Then she changed color and changed back again.

"I don't understand," she said, hesitatingly, "why—I mean what difference it made."

"Difference," exclaimed Captain Eli. "It
was all the difference between a man on deck
and a man overboard—that's the difference it
was to me. I didn't expect to be talkin' to
you so early this Christmas mornin', but
things has been sprung on me, and I can't
help it. I just want to ask you one thing:
Did you think I was gettin' up this Christmas-tree and the Christmas dinner and the
whole business for the good of the little gal,
and for the good of you, and for the good of
Captain Cephas?"

Mrs. Trimmer had now recovered a very
fair possession of herself. "Of course I did,"
she answered, looking up at him as she spoke.
"Who else could it have been for?"

"Well," said he, "you were mistaken. It
wasn't for any one of you; it was all for me—
for my own self."

"You yourself?" said she. "I don't see
how."

"But I see how," he answered. "It's been
a long time since I wanted to speak my mind
to you, Mrs. Trimmer, but I didn't ever have
no chance; and all these Christmas doin's

was got up to give me the chance not only of speakin' to you, but of showin' my colors better than I could show them in any other way; and everything went on a-skimmin' till this mornin', when that stranger that we brought in from the shoal piped up and asked for you. Then I went overboard—at least I thought I did—and sunk down, down, clean out of soundin's."

"That was too bad, Captain," said she, speaking very gently, "after all your trouble and kindness."

"But I don't know now," he continued, "whether I went overboard or whether I am on deck. Can you tell me, Mrs. Trimmer?"

She looked up at him; her eyes were very soft, and her lips trembled just a little. "It seems to me, Captain," she said, "that you are on deck—if you want to be."

The captain stepped closer to her. "Mrs. Trimmer," said he, "is that brother of yours comin' back?"

"Yes," she answered, surprised at the sudden question. "He's just gone up to the store to buy a shirt and some things. He got himself splashed trying to push his boat off last night."

"Well, then," said Captain Eli, "would you mind tellin' him when he comes back that you and me's engaged to be married? I don't know whether I've made a mistake in the lights or not, but would you mind tellin' him that?"

Mrs. Trimmer looked at him. Her eyes were not so soft as they had been, but they were brighter. "I'd rather you'd tell him that yourself," said she.

The little girl sat on the floor near the Christmas tree, just finishing a large piece of red-and-white candy which she had taken out of her stocking. "People do hug a lot at Christmas-time," said she to herself. Then she drew out a piece of blue-and-white candy and began on that.

Captain Cephas waited a long time for his friend to return, and at last he thought it would be well to go and look for him. When he entered the house he found Mrs. Trimmer sitting on the sofa in the parlor, with Captain Eli on one side of her and her brother on the other, and each of them holding one of her hands.

"It looks as if I was in port, don't it?" said Captain Eli to his astonished friend. "Well, here I am, and here's my fust mate," inclining his head toward Mrs. Trimmer. "And she's in port too, safe and sound; and that strange captain on the other side of her, he's her brother Bob, who's been away for years and years, and is just home from Madagascar."

"Singapore," amended brother Bob.

Captain Cephas looked from one to the other of the three occupants of the sofa, but made no immediate remark. Presently a smile of genial maliciousness stole over his face, and he asked, "How about the poor little gal? Have you sent her back to Mrs. Crumley's?"

The little girl came out from behind the Christmas tree, her stocking, now but half filled, in her hand. "Here I am," she said. "Don't you want to give me a Christmas hug, Captain Cephas? You and me's the only ones that hasn't had any."

The Christmas dinner was as truly and perfectly a sailor-cooked meal as ever was served on board a ship or off it. Captain Cephas had said that, and when he had so spoken there was no need of further words.

It was nearly dark that afternoon, and they were all sitting around the kitchen fire, the three seafaring men smoking, and Mrs. Trimmer greatly enjoying it. There could be no objection to the smell of tobacco in this house so long as its future mistress enjoyed it. The little girl sat on the floor nursing a Chinese idol which had been one of her presents.

"After all," said Captain Eli, meditatively, "this whole business come out of my sleepin' with my best ear up; for if I'd slept with my hard-o'-hearin' ear up—" Mrs. Trimmer put one finger on his lips. "All right," said Captain Eli, " I won't say no more; but it would have been different."

Even now, several years after that Christmas, when there is no Mrs. Trimmer, and the little girl, who has been regularly adopted by Captain Eli and his wife, is studying geography, and knows more about latitude and longitude than her teacher at school, Captain Eli has still a slight superstitious dread of sleeping with his best ear uppermost.

"Of course it's the most all-fired nonsense," he says to himself over and over again. Nevertheless, he feels safer when it is his "hard-o'-hearin' ear" that is not upon the pillow.

AS ONE WOMAN TO ANOTHER

AS ONE WOMAN TO ANOTHER

IT was a beautiful, quiet August morning and I lay in a hammock looking up at the blue and cloudless sky. The hammock was hung between two trees on the back lawn of my father's country house. A few hundred feet to the right the roof and chimneys of the house rose above the tree tops. At the foot of the lawn, not quite so far away, a little river ran. I could not see it, but now and then I heard the gurgle of the water, and this, with the singing and chirping of the birds and the occasional chatter of a red squirrel in a tree near by, were all the sounds I heard upon that quiet morning.

Gazing upward past the nearest tree tops I saw against the sky a little black spot. This was odd and I waved my hand in front of my face, thinking it might be some fly or insect near me, but it was nothing of the kind. It was a spot in the sky. I moved

my head from side to side but I could see it
only in ono place. It was not the effect of
disordered vision, it was not fancy, it was
really a spot against the sky.

I sat up in my hammock and gazed steadfastly at the distant speck, and as I looked I
could see that it was growing larger. In less
than ten minutes I saw that it was a balloon,
and that it was slowly approaching in my direction, and also descending. I ran out on
the open lawn to get a better view of it.
There was a very gentle wind, and this blew
directly in my face as I looked at the balloon.
I believed that it would pass over the lawn.

I became very much interested, even excited, and the more so because I now perceived that it was a small balloon, entirely
too small to sustain the weight of a man. If
it had been an ordinary balloon with an oc-
cupant, it might have been interesting to hail
him as he passed over my head, but here was
something that came floating out of the sky
toward me, and which I might secure as a
prize if I could follow it until it came to
earth.

Nearer and nearer it approached, and I
could plainly see the little basket which hung

beneath the partly distended bag. The wild desire seized me to capture this air-ship. As I hastily considered my chances they did not appear encouraging. The wind, though light, was steady, and there was every reason to believe that the balloon would be carried across the river, and might not touch the earth until it had gone a long distance on the other side. If I crossed the river I might be able to keep up with the balloon, but I suddenly remembered that this would be impossible because my younger brother Richard had gone fishing in the boat. He had started to fly a kite I had made him, but the wind had not been strong enough and he had taken to the water.

As I hurried down to the river I could not see or hear the boat, but by the wall at the bottom of the lawn I saw Richard's kite, and near by a basket in which he kept his fishing tackle. A thought struck me; I ran down to the wall and turned over the basket and spread its contents on the ground. Among them I found three large fish-hooks which the youngster had used at the seashore. Then I sprang to the kite; the wind was fresher now. With all the nervous earnestness of a boy I bound the three hooks, back to back and

points downward, to the cord a few feet below
the point where it was fastened to the kite,
and then, the kite in one hand, and the ball
of cord in the other, I ran out into the open
and looked up. Not far away, on the other
side of the house, but still high above the
tree tops, I saw the balloon steadily moving
toward me. It would certainly cross the
river, it might sail on for hours. I set the
kite against the wind; I tossed it up; I ran.
In a few seconds it caught the breeze, steadied
itself and began to rise. On I ran toward the
house, and higher and higher rose the kite.
If I could only get it high enough; if I could
hook it on to that balloon I should be as
happy as a deer stalker who brings down
a stag.

The kite went up grandly, high over the
river, higher and higher, and I ran this way
and that to bring it in line with the balloon.
I let out more cord; the kite, like a hawk,
was now soaring far above its quarry. If I
could bring the cord against the balloon; if
those hooks would catch; if they would take
such good hold of some of the netting or of
the basket so that I might pull it down! In
my excitement and with my eyes ever aloft, I

fell over a little bush, but it did not matter; I was up in an instant and the kite made but a few flaps before I had it steady again.

The balloon had now passed over my head and was not far from the cord. I ran a few steps to the right and then pulled down. The cord almost touched it. I pulled down harder. I could feel a little thump upon the cord and then the balloon moved gently away from the kite.

I let out more cord and ran toward the river. The kite rose again. I pulled it down. With eyes fixed as though I were aiming a rifle I moved the cord so that it might again touch the balloon. It did touch; I pulled it sharply; the hooks caught in the netting over the bag and held! What a bound my heart gave! Had I been my young brother I could not have breathed more triumphantly.

But I had not yet secured my prize. The cord, though light, was a strong one, but there was now a great strain upon it. Although the balloon was small, with the bag but partly filled with gas, it presented a considerable surface to the wind, and I soon began to fear that the cord would break before I could pull down both the balloon and the kite, but in a moment I saw that the bag was collapsing, and the strain upon the cord was becoming much less. I could easily imagine what had happened. One or more of the hooks had torn the silk of the balloon, and as gas escaped through the rent it was falling by its own weight.

Down, down it came, pulling the kite with it, and all I had to do was to draw in the cord and direct my descending prize toward an open spot where it would not catch on the boughs of trees.

Still down it came, and as if I had pulled in an aërial fish, I soon beheld the whole affair lying on the grass at my feet.

For a moment I stood and gazed, but in the whole jumbled mass I paid attention to nothing but a small basket with a piece of waterproof cloth tied over the top. I approached it and then I stopped to consider. I felt a strong desire to inspect the secret of that basket alone. Fortunately my mother and father were away and my sister had gone to visit some neighbors. Richard was boating, but he might return at any moment. I jerked out my knife and cut the basket loose from the cords, and then, taking it under my arm, I ran to the house and up-stairs to my room, where I locked myself in.

With trembling hands and eager curiosity I removed the cover from the basket. The first thing I saw was a small cage containing a pigeon. I took this out and set it on the floor, the bird cooing and turning itself around as if it were glad to see a human being. Then I perceived a wooden framework, in which were set some instruments, thermometers, barometers, and I do not know what. On the top of this was attached a stout envelope on which was written: "To the person who finds this balloon."

It took me but a few seconds to release the envelope. It was not sealed and I opened it and drew out a letter. This surprised me. As soon as I had noticed the instruments securely fastened to the framework I had suspected that this balloon had been sent up by some scientific person and that the envelope contained technical directions to the finder. But here was a letter on two sheets of cream-colored note paper, and evidently written by a lady. I glanced at the end of it. It had no signature, and then, still seated on the floor, I read it:

"Whoever you may be who shall find this letter I beg and implore you to read it carefully and then to do what you can to assist a fellow-being who can ask no one in the world but yourself to help her. I cannot write everything in this letter, but I will put in all that I can. I am an unfortunate girl who is suffering great misery, and who is cut off from all the world by a cruelty which would take a long time to describe. All I can say here is that my uncle, who has been appointed my guardian and the trustee of my property, has kept me for months and months and months as a close prisoner. I never go off the premises and I never see anybody but him and one or two servants. I am not allowed to send any letters that are not first examined by him, and my situation is getting to be more dreadful every day.

"It will not be long before I shall go crazy. I have tried ever so many ways of getting news of my situation to somebody in the outside world, but I have failed, and now I try this, which is my last chance. My uncle is a very learned man and is always making experiments. He sends up balloons with instruments in them, which register heat and

cold and height, and all sorts of things. He
always puts in his balloon a letter to the person who shall find it when it comes down,
asking that person to look at the instruments
and set down whatever they register. He
also tells him to take out the pigeon which is
in the cage and remove from its wing a roll
of very thin paper. Then he asks that the
registrations be written on this paper, and
that it shall be tied on the pigeon's wing just
as it was before; after which the pigeon is to
be set at liberty, when it will immediately
fly back to him. He also sends his address
and requests that a letter be written to him
giving all sorts of information on a printed
form which he incloses. But he wants the
pigeon sent first, because the balloon may
come down at some place which is very far
from a post-office.

"My plan is this, and if you get this letter you will know that it has succeeded. He
sends up his balloons from a courtyard
which is under my window, and one of the
first things he does is to tie his letter to the
instrument frame, and the last thing he does
is to go and get the pigeon. While he is
away doing this I shall slip down to the

court, take out his letter and put in mine, and then pray that it may go to some good soul who will help me.

"What I want you to do is this: first make up your mind whether or not you are willing to help a poor unfortunate girl, shut off from all other help by a sky above her which she cannot reach, an earth below her which she cannot penetrate, and walls all about her which she cannot get through. If you are willing to do what you can for me please take the paper from the pigeon's wing and write your name and address upon it, and then tie it on as it was before. But if you are not willing to help me, and do not wish to put yourself to trouble by meddling in the affairs of an utter stranger, please at least be kind enough not to write anything on the paper which might let my uncle know what I have done, but let the pigeon come back just as it is.

"I am almost sure it will come to me before he sees it, for I have fed this bird for a long time on the balcony under my window, and I shall watch for it by day and by night. But if my uncle should get it first he will see nothing but your address or the empty paper, and so he will not know what I have done. If I first get the pigeon and find your name on it, I will immediately write to you, asking you to send me some drawing material or something of that kind, and give my name and address. That sort of letter my uncle will let pass. I do not send my address now because I am afraid to do so until I really know of some person who is willing I should send it.

"Now when you get my note I implore you to come to the little town where I live and find out where my uncle's house is. You can easily do this, for everybody knows him. Then please, I beg of you, try to see me. There is a large garden at the back of the house and a high wall all around it. After I hear from you I shall be there as much as I can. You cannot make a mistake, for I am the only young person in the house. Even if it should rain I will go out with a mackintosh. And now, without knowing who you are, I put my happiness, my fortune, and I may even say the possession of my senses, into your charge, for I know if you will make my situation known to the proper persons I shall soon be free and happy."

For a long time after I read this letter I sat on the floor holding it in my hand. What a message to come to me out of the clear August sky! How glad I was that nobody but myself had seen the balloon, and that I could sit here and consider the matter without interference. While thinking thus I was reminded that I was not alone, and that there was another party who had an interest in the proceedings. This was the pigeon, who began to coo louder and louder and to turn itself around with considerable vigor.

I laid down the letter and picked up the cage, and as I put my hand under it to raise it, so that I could better look at the pigeon's wing, I felt that the bottom of the cage was very warm, and on examining it I found that the bottom was a double one and contained a long bag of fine charcoal, which, on being lighted at one end, would burn for many hours, after the manner of the little Japanese stoves. This, no doubt, was to protect the pigeon against the extreme cold of high altitudes. The wicked uncle must indeed be an ingenious and practical man.

I did not look at the instruments; my

mind was too much excited by the letter to allow me to examine their registrations. I was entirely occupied with the question: "What shall I do for the writer of this letter?" I could not believe it was a hoax because no one wishing to play a joke would send up such a balloon with those expensive instruments.

I thought for a moment of waiting until some of the family returned, and taking counsel of them, but this idea I quickly rejected. If I were going to do anything I ought to do it now. If there really should be a young woman who needed help she was waiting and watching for the return of that pigeon. If it should prove to be nothing but a joke I would rather be laughed at for doing what I thought was a good action than to have my conscience reproach me for being a coward, afraid of being laughed at.

Now that my decision was made I drew the pigeon from the cage, took off the paper, noticing how it was rolled and tied, wrote on it my name and address, attached it again to the wing of the bird, and then, going to the window, threw the pigeon into the air. For a few minutes it flew round and round, then it mounted high and disappeared over the tops of the trees.

"It has gone to her," I said, and I sat down and read the letter over again.

Suddenly I thought of the balloon on the grass. Why should any one know of this thing but myself, at least until I chose to make it known? I ran down to the lawn and disengaged the kite, and then, rolling up the balloon-bag with its netting, I carried it to a corner of the grounds and concealed it under a heavy hedge. Then I took Richard's kite to the river-wall and restored all his possessions to the condition in which I had found them.

Now all traces of my messenger from the sky having been removed and my answer to the message having been despatched, I sat upon the wall to think more about it, and while doing so my mind became deeply, and, I may say, not altogether pleasantly, impressed by the remembrance that I was engaged to be married. This, of course, had never been anything but a most delightful remembrance, but just now it did not seem to fit into the condition of things. Perhaps I ought to have remembered it sooner.

GOING TO THE WINDOW, I THREW THE PIGEON INTO THE AIR.

What would Clara Markham think of my offering to become the knight-errant for the benefit of another young lady? That this lady's name and habitation were unknown would make no difference, and if it should prove that no such lady existed it would still make no difference, for I had assumed her to be a real person, suffering real hardships, and had, in fact, offered myself as her protector. The more I thought of Clara Markham in connection with what I had done the more my thoughts troubled me. One thing was clear to me: I had no right to keep this affair a secret from her. So, that afternoon, I rode over to her father's house, about two miles distant, and being fortunate enough to find Clara at home, I conducted her to a secluded spot on the ground, and there I astonished her as I think she was never astonished before. With her eyes very wide open she sat and looked at me.

"If it had been anybody but you, Tom," she exclaimed, "had told me this, I would not have believed it! I would not have believed there had been any balloon, any pigeon, any letter. But what you tell me, I believe, no matter what it is."

To this I replied properly and added that I expected her always to do so.

"But there is one thing I do not believe," she went on to say, "and that is that there is any young lady at all in the matter, or if there is that she is in trouble and needs assistance. I think it is all a hoax, and we need not consider it or talk about it any more."

"But, my dear girl," said I, "I have sent my name to the writer of that letter, and in so doing I have given her a promise that I will help her. Of course it all may be a hoax, but suppose it is not, would you like to think that I had positively declined to help a fellow-being in distress? Would you like to consider me that sort of a man?"

"Of course not," said Clara. "If she is a real person and needs help she ought to be helped, but there are other people besides you who can do it."

"Who, for instance?" I asked.

"There is my cousin Charles," she said.

Now, above all people in this world I hated that cousin Charles. He was in the habit of mingling with the Markham family as if he belonged to it, and I had often been jealous of him in regard to Clara, and now it seemed as if I were even more jealous of him in regard to this unknown girl, to whom, perhaps, the pigeon had, even now, carried my message.

"No," said I, a little too decidedly perchance, "your cousin would not do. I have sent my name in good faith, and whatever happens I shall act in a straightforward and honest way, telling you everything that I do and taking your advice about it. But your cousin would either make fun of the whole affair or else—anyway it would, in fact, be a breach of confidence for me to pass over the management of this affair to anyone else until the writer of that letter should authorize me to do so. I found the balloon; I am the person to whom she wrote, that is to say" (here a happy thought struck me) "you and I are the persons to whom she wrote, and it is to us that she appeals for help. Now, are we going to throw her over even before we know who she is?"

At this Clara's countenance began to clear a little.

"That is true," she said; "you and I are the persons who have this case in our hands."

"And whatever happens we will keep the whole matter a secret between ourselves," I said.

It was three days after this conversation that, walking on the lawn, I saw our man bringing the mail-bag from the post-office. As had happened on the two preceding mornings I met him at the gate and looked into the bag to see if there were any letters for me. This morning there were several letters addressed to me, and among them one in the handwriting of the balloon lady. I put this in my pocket and tore open the others, but I am sure I did not know then, nor have I ever since known, what was in them. I went to my room and opened my letter. As I did so I said to myself that I ought not to be so interested in this correspondence. But I was interested—so much so that I cut my finger with the knife with which I opened the envelope.

The following is an exact copy of the note I read:

August 17, 1891.

Mr. Thomas W. Grant,

Dear Sir:—Having seen your advertisement of music for the guitar I beg you will send me the pieces Nos. 39,

102 and 68. I inclose a postal note for the amount, ninety-five cents.

> Yours truly,
> GRACE SOMERVILLE ROSLEY,

Care George R. Rosley, Esq.,
> Wolverton, Hunterdon Co.,
> > New Jersey.

"Well! well!" said I, "she is as practical-minded as her uncle. Think of her putting in that postal note! What a capital idea! The most suspicious person would never imagine that this letter had been sent to one whom she had called upon to act as her protector, her knight-errant. Of course the pigeon went to her first, for had her uncle received my address there would have been no reason for his giving it to her. Everything has gone well, and now what am I to do?" As I asked myself this question my conscience again reproached me for taking so much interest in the matter, but I turned severely on my conscience and asked it, in turn, if it were not possible for a man to truly love one woman and yet feel desirous of helping another woman in sore distress? If these two things were incompatible, no man should love. At this, I am happy to say, my conscience was completely humbled and said no more.

But when I took the note I had received to Clara she said a great deal. She took much interest in the matter, even more, I thought, than I did, and in my opinion entirely too much.

"I believe," said she, "that the writer of this is a person accustomed to deception. I do not see how she could bring herself to say she had seen your advertisement, and then to send you money! It is a positive insult! How much better it would have been if she had written plainly and honestly what she had to say, without all these tricks."

With a sigh at the obtuseness of the female intellect I explained to Clara that if Miss Rosley had written a plain, straightforward letter her uncle would not have allowed her to send it. Nothing but a simple business note like this would have passed his suspicious scrutiny. The inclosing of the postal note was—I was about to say a stroke of genius, but I changed this expression to—the most prudent thing possible.

"When a person is a prisoner and guarded with cruel watchfulness," I said, "subterfuges are necessary and right. Would you hesitate if you were cruelly imprisoned, and wished

to communicate with me, to resort to a sub-
terfuge ? "

" I do not believe in such imprisonments
in this enlightened age, and in this country,"
said she; "it is nonsense to suppose that
there are such things."

" It does seem so," I answered, " but everything is possible, and supposing that this
young lady's story should be true, how could
we reconcile it to our consciences if we totally
disregard her second appeal to us for help?"

Clara did not immediately answer. Her
mind seemed disturbed.

" Of course she ought to be helped," she
said, "but you are not the person to do it.
Why couldn't I go to her and hear what she
has to say ? "

"You!" said I. "Impossible. Wolverton
is a long way from here, and, besides, you
could not go about alone asking for Mr.
Rosley's house, and even manage to get an
undisturbed interview with his niece."

" I would rather do that than have you do
it," she said, "but it is not necessary for me
to go alone. Cousin Charles could go with
me."

" If your cousin goes," said I, a little sharply, for this remark annoyed me very much, "he would better go by himself. But I do not want him to have anything to do with it. This is my affair."

"And mine," said she.

"Yes," I assented, "it is ours. But," I added, "although I came to you with it and laid the whole thing before you exactly as I knew it myself, trusting you as I always do in everything, you do not seem in the least willing to trust me."

At this Clara's eyes became a little dim. "Tom," she said, putting her hand on my arm, "you have no right to say that." And then for ten minutes our conversation became strictly personal. When this interchange of sentiments had been satisfactorily concluded, Clara suddenly exclaimed:

"Tell me, Tom, what it is that you think you ought to do. Have you thought of any plan?"

"It is all as simple as can be," I answered; "there is no plan but one. I go to Wolverton and I find out where Mr. Rosley's house is. Then I walk toward it and around the back of it, on some elevated ground where I can look over the wall, for, of course, if there

were not such a place she could not expect
any one to see her in the garden, and then if
I see a young lady I will approach the garden
and speak to her, probably through a grated
gate. I will ask her to tell me her story as
quickly as possible, and, after making some
inquiries in the village, by which, without exciting suspicion, I can find out something about the Rosley family, I will return
to you and tell you all about it. Then we
can decide whether or not we ought to inform the legal authorities or her distant
friends, if she has any, of the state of her
case, or let the whole thing drop."

"You must have been thinking a great deal
about it," she said quickly, "to have such a
plan as that so pat and ready to carry out.
But I am not going to find fault with you; I
know you have one of the quickest of minds.
Of course your plan is the proper one, and I
would approve of it in every way if it were
Mr. Rosley's nephew who was imprisoned, but
a young girl in a sequestered garden, that is
dreadfully different!"

I replied loftily, "To me she would be
simply a human being—her sex, her age, her
appearance would be nothing to me. I would

consider only her sufferings, and would not even consider my ability to relieve her. I would consult you about that."

"Tom," said Clara, "I do not suppose that I really can go to talk to that girl, which is what I want to do, but do you think that you could go to her as I would, feeling all the time that you were filling my place, and that you could speak to her, and listen to her, as one woman to another?"

I did not hesitate a moment. "Clara!" I exclaimed, "I believe that I could."

"Then, Tom," said the noble girl, "you can go."

There was no chance to say or do more, for we saw persons approaching from the house.

The next morning I took an early train for Wolverton. I determined to be very cautious about this business, and if I should find there were no Mr. Rosley, and consequently no young lady in a garden, I would quietly return without giving anyone a chance to make fun of me.

Wolverton was a small village, and as I took some refreshments at the inn I asked some very natural questions of the innkeeper

WHILE THE INN-KEEPER WAS GIVING ME THE INFORMATION I ENDEAVORED TO SUPPRESS MY EXCITEMENT.

about the village and some of its principal residents.

I was disappointed that he did not mention the only name I cared to hear, but on my remarking that I had heard a scientific gentleman lived in the place, he answered:

"Oh, you must mean Mr. Rosley, but he doesn't live in the village. His house is about a mile out."

"In what direction?" I asked, carelessly, and while the innkeeper was giving me the information I endeavored to suppress the excitement caused by the knowledge that I was really on the right track.

As soon as I could decently do so I paid my little bill and sauntered out. I know the man took me for a book agent, but I was very well satisfied that he should do so.

The Rosley place was an old-fashioned one. The house faced the main road, but stood well back from it, and a narrow lane, at right angles with the main road, passed the house at no great distance, and as I walked along this lane I could see through a bushy hedge a courtyard, lying in an angle of the mansion.

"That is the place where he sends up his

balloons," I said to myself; "her window must look out on it."

Passing still farther on my heart fairly bounded when I perceived behind the house the high wall of a garden.

As I passed the long side wall I saw that it had no gate nor opening, and when I reached the end of it I found that the garden backed upon a field planted with corn. On the outside of the back wall was a row of cedar-trees.

Looking about me and finding that no one was in sight I got into the cornfield and approached the garden. I passed along the whole of the back wall but found no door nor grating. I peeped around the corner to the other side and saw there was a door there but it was of solid plank and too near the house. When my unknown correspondent wrote to me that I would see her in the garden, it evidently had not entered her head to inform me how I should see her. The neighboring elevation from which I had imagined I might look down into the garden did not exist, and the only way in which I could see into it was to look over the back wall, where I would myself be protected from observation.

This would not be difficult if I could manage to climb into one of the cedar-trees which stood on the outer side of the wall.

The position in which I found myself while I was quietly surveying Mr. Rosley's walled garden, with the intention of getting into it if I could do so, was not altogether satisfactory. I felt as if I were engaged in a sly and underhand business. Clandestine methods are allowable in war and love, but I was not engaged in either of these pursuits, besides I was endeavoring to speak to a young lady as a woman would speak to her. Would a woman have climbed into a tree to talk with her?

However, I could not burden my mind with such casuistries. I had come to do a thing and I must do it.

I quietly climbed into a tree and very cautiously projected my head above the wall. I looked into a garden with flower-beds, paths bordered with high rows of box, masses of shrubbery here and there, and a heavily shaded arbor, but I saw no human being. Some of the branches of the tree in which I was standing rested on the top of the wall so that I looked through them without danger

of being seen. I looked and I looked and I
looked, but there was nothing I cared to see
and my heart grew heavier and heavier. At
one time I thought of going boldly to the
front door and asking for Miss Rosley. I
might thus, at least, find out if such a person
existed, and if this were so I might even
manage in the presence of witnesses to talk
to her about the music she had ordered and
thus let her know who I was.

Suddenly, and with such startling effect
that I almost slipped out of the tree, there
appeared before me an apparition. It was
that of a young lady dressed in white, and
she came out of the summer-house. She held
a book in her hand, and with sparkling eyes
and lips half open she stepped rapidly toward
me. Stopping a little distance from the wall,
she said :

"Is that Mr. Thomas ——? If so, what
is the rest of your name ? "

I could scarcely answer, so surprised was
I. The girl was beautiful. I do not believe
I ever saw such eyes. Clara's are dark.

"W. Grant," said I.

A smile of delight spread over her face.
She was not tall, but her movements and ex-

"IS THAT MR. THOMAS ——?"

pressions had a charm in them which seemed
entirely novel to me.

"Oh, I am so glad," she said; "I had not
the least idea there was anybody here until I
happened to look up from my book and saw
those branches moving. Then I noticed your
hat. How good of you to come. Do you
think you can reach this?" Then dropping
her book on the ground she took from her
pocket a letter and held it up to me. "That
is a full account of me, with all things which
I wish to have known. I give it to you now
because if anyone should come before I have
time to talk to you, you will not have to go
away without knowing everything."

I leaned over the wall, stretched down my
arm and took the letter.

"Then I may talk to you?" I said.

"Oh, yes," she answered, "there are a
good many things I want to ask you. If I
had something to stand on it would be better," and she looked about her.

"Oh, you need not trouble yourself to
stand on anything," said I, visions of top-
pling boxes or barrels coming into my mind.
"May I not get over the wall and speak with
you on the ground?"

"That would be better," she said, "but I am so afraid that if anyone should come you could not get back again."

I glanced along the inner side of the wall; not far away there was a low pear-tree, and from a crotch of this I saw I could readily reach the coping.

"I can get back again easily enough," said I, and in a moment I was standing by her side.

"Let us step into the arbor," she said; "it is possible that we may be seen here from the house."

I followed her quick steps toward the arbor.

"Now let us sit down here," said she, "and not speak very loud. I am dreadfully anxious to ask you some things, and, besides, I can tell you what is in that letter a great deal better than I have written it. But first of all I want to ask you some questions. Have you a sister?"

"Yes."

"What is her name?"

"Margaret."

"Oh, and is your mother living, and what was her name before she was married?"

"Margaret also—Margaret Carson."

She clasped her little hands in her lap, and turned herself slowly toward me.

"Then you are not the person," said she.

"What person?" I asked in consternation.

"When my father was living," she said, "he had a partner who was his great friend, and although I am not positively and certainly sure that his name was the same as yours, I know it was Grant, and I think it was Thomas W. He is dead, but I know he had a son whose name was Thomas, and I thought there was no reason why he should not be living at the address you sent me. But I know his sister and his mother, and her maiden name was Stanfield, and neither of them is named Margaret. Ever since I have been in trouble I have so longed to know where the Grants lived, and when I took your address from the pigeon's wing I could have screamed with delight. But, after all, you are not the person."

Did this mean that I was to get up and retire over the garden wall? I could not act on such a supposition.

"I do not know any Grants who married

Stanfields," said I, speaking very earnestly, "but I assure you, Miss Rosley, that that does not make the least difference in the world. You want help and I am here. Tell me what it is that I can do for you, and it shall be done just the same as if I were the son of your father's friend. I judged from the letter that I found in the balloon that you were in great trouble. Now, I am a lawyer, tell me everything, and it may be I can help you as well as anyone else. Your appeal for help came to me floating out of the sky, and it made a great impression upon me. I felt that such a call as that must not be disregarded. I came to you just as soon as it was possible, and now I do not want you to send me away without allowing me to do what I can for you."

"How glad I am you are a lawyer," she said, the light again shining in her eyes. "A lawyer ought to know exactly what to do, and it was wonderfully kind of you to take so much trouble for an absolute stranger, and now I will begin at the beginning and tell you everything as quickly as I can."

The story she told did not surprise me. In fact, I had guessed the drift of it. She was an orphan and had reason to believe that her uncle, who was her guardian, and who of late years had become very eccentric, had spent a great part, or perhaps all, of her fortune in his expensive experiments, and since she had left school and was of age he had been very suspicious and watchful of her, refusing her permission to travel or visit her friends, and lately had actually instituted a system of espionage of all her correspondence. There was no doubt that he was afraid she would write something or say something that would cause an investigation of her affairs before he had finished a great scientific work on which he was engaged, and from which, as he informed her almost every day, he expected to derive great profit as well as reputation.

Miss Rosley's affection for her uncle, whose mind was probably unsettled, had prevented her from appealing to the neighbors, by whom the old gentleman was evidently much disliked, and who had already talked about the strictness with which he treated his niece, although they did not know the extent of his vigilance. Such an appeal, my companion said, would probably have resulted in his being sent to a lunatic asylum or a prison, and she had, therefore, confined herself to efforts to

open a correspondence with the outside world.
If she could not in this way bring her case
to the knowledge of friends, she might, at
least, obtain the assistance of an unpreju-
diced and dispassionate lawyer, who, without
making her uncle the subject of public scandal, would quietly obtain for her an allowance sufficient for her support, and let her
uncle keep the rest. Thus, under legal pro-
tection, she would get out into the world and
seek her friends, leaving her uncle to go on
with his experiments and expenses without
fear of disturbance from her. If he could be
sure that he were in no danger of an investigation of his guardianship he would be quite
willing, she believed, to let her go wherever
she chose.

I did not interrupt her story. It was told
with great directness and clearness, owing, no
doubt, to her having previously written it.

"Now," said she, when she had finished,
"you are a lawyer; will you take my case,
will you advise me?"

"Most gladly will I do that," I said. "I
will take counsel of the heads of the law firm
with which I am connected. I will manage
the matter in the quietest and most private

way, mentioning no names until it is necessary. You may suppose that I have not had
experience enough to conduct an affair which
demands such delicacy, prudence, and knowledge, but I assure you that the firm of Round-
man, Bostwick & Unger stands in the highest
rank of the profession. I will remember all
that you have told me, and I will carefully
study the paper you have given me. I will
find the family of your father's partner. I
will put you into communication with them,
for I can manage a correspondence for you.
In fact, I will attend to anything you wish."

"That is very good of you," she said. "I
believe that lawyers are as kind as doctors.
When I succeeded in getting my letter into the
balloon, I really had great hopes that something would come of it, but I did not believe
that I would so soon have the chance of
speaking to a lawyer and putting my affairs
into his hands. I think it is wonderful."

"I consider it one of the lucky chances of
my life," said I, "that I happened to be the
one who discovered that balloon."

"It was a happy thing for me," she said,
"for you came so quickly. Now there is
something I have just thought of. Wouldn't

it be well, before you do anything else, to find out where the Grants live—I mean my Grants; then, if when my uncle first hears from you or your firm, he should become excited and angry, so that I should be afraid of him—and there have been times when I have been a little afraid of him—I might quietly escape from this place and go to the Grants?"

This proposition alarmed me. "My dear young lady," I replied, "if you suspect any such danger as that we must all be very careful. In no event must you try to get away from here without assistance. Any attempt of the kind would be extremely hazardous, for your uncle will be extraordinarily watchful, and in his state of mind there is no knowing what might happen, and in any case you must not travel by yourself. Don't think of doing anything of the sort without my knowing it. It may be well for me to stay near you after negotiations have been opened with your uncle. I can take lodgings in the village and we can arrange signals, so that if you think you ought to leave this house I shall be ready to take you wherever you want to go. If your Grants are too far away

I will take you to my Grants. My mother and sister will be glad to receive you."

"How good you are," she said, and she held out her hand. I took it and did not immediately release it. I think she supposed that this was because I wished to take leave of her.

"Good-by," she said, as she gently withdrew her hand, "good-by; I shall think of other things to say to you, of course, but I ought not to keep you any longer, and somebody might come out before you could get over the wall."

I did not want to go; I was not at that moment afraid of anyone. I was sure I had not thought of all the things I ought to say. Happily one of these things now came to me.

"I will tell you what you ought to do," I said. "You should write a letter to your Grants; then I can give it to them if I see them, or send it to them even if they are in California or abroad. Now is your chance to communicate with your friends."

"But I cannot write a letter before you go," said she.

"Oh, I will leave you and come back again

this afternoon. Then you can give me the letter."

"I shall not say anything more about your kindness," said she, "because there is so much of it. About three o'clock will be a good time, and do not show yourself unless you see me."

She raised a little watch that was dangling at her belt, and looked at it.

"Dear me!" she exclaimed, "it is after one o'clock. I had not the least idea it was so late."

She rose, and as I perceived that she wanted to see me safely off before she went to the house, I assured her that I would be back at three, and jumping into the pear-tree easily cleared the wall.

I went back to the inn for my luncheon.

"Did you see all the people I told you the names of?" said my host.

"No," said I, "but I shall stay here for the rest of the day."

"You didn't get out to old Rosley's, I suppose," he continued; "but it wouldn't be much use unless you've got books about balloons or stars."

"I may get out there this afternoon," said

I, thinking it well to divert suspicion if my course should be noticed.

At about a quarter before three I was in the cedar-tree looking over the garden wall. It was a long time before I saw her coming, and then in a moment I was in the garden. She hurried toward me.

"It wasn't necessary to get over the wall," she said. "I am so afraid you will be seen. I thought you would reach down and take the letter. But now that you are here, please come into the arbor. You cannot be seen from the house there. Here is a letter to Mrs. Grant; perhaps you would like to look over it. I shall have to ask you to hurry, for my uncle is in a very bad way to-day. He was angry because I was two minutes late to lunch, and he may send for me or come for me at any minute. He was greatly disturbed when he found his pigeon without anything on its wing, and has since been expecting a letter from the finder, and as none has come he is very cross and out of humor with all the world."

I had no time to waste in reading her letter. I glanced over it and told her that no doubt she had stated everything correctly, and that

I would see that it reached Mrs. Grant if she were alive. Then I stood and looked down on that beautiful young face, not happy as it had been in the morning, but troubled and anxious. I could not bear to go away and leave her with this half-crazy and selfish old man. It was not safe, it was not right, that she should be here. Earnestly and quickly I told her what I thought.

She looked up at me with tears in her eyes and seemed about to speak when suddenly she started.

"Hark!" said she, "I think my uncle is calling me. Yes, he is."

At this instant there came a loud call, or, rather, shout, from the house. She turned pale.

"It is not like him to do that. I must run," she said, "or he will be here. Let me go, and then hurry away as fast as you can."

I had seized her by the arm to detain her an instant. "I shall not go," I said quickly, "I shall stay behind the garden wall until I know you are not in danger. When you have a chance come out and let me know; I shall be there."

She raised her eyes to mine without a word and then she fled.

I sat on the ground at the back of the wall, listening. The place was so secluded that if no one had come into the cornfield, and there was no agricultural reason why anyone should do so at this time of the year, I might have camped there for a week. I was afraid to stand in a tree, for fear I might move the branches, but from where I was I thought I could hear the lightest footstep or the faintest call. After a time I took out my watch and looked at it.

It was nearly four o'clock. Almost immediately after that a little gravel stone came over the wall and fell down near me. Instantly I was in the tree looking over the wall. She stood almost beneath me.

"Hush!" she whispered. "Do not get over the wall nor speak. I heard the click of your watch and knew you must be there. Get down again and wait, please."

I obeyed her implicitly. I did not even hesitate long enough to see what she did.

I do not know how long I waited, but suddenly I was startled by footsteps on the outside of the wall, and looking around I saw Miss Rosley approaching me. Her face was pale as she put her finger on her lips.

"I will go through the corn," she whispered, "to the end of the field. Meet me there." And without another word she disappeared between two rows of tall, waving green blades.

For a moment I stood, not knowing what to do. It was plain she did not wish me to follow her, and as I did not know the extent or conformation of the cornfield, I thought it best to go out to the lane and so keep on a parallel course with her. The cornfield was a large one, and when I came to the end of it I found a piece of wooded land with a little stream running under the trees. I got over a rough stone wall and pushed my way through the underbrush and ferns to the spot which I supposed was as far from the lane as the point where Miss Rosley entered the field.

I had not misjudged the distance. Soon I saw a speck of white and then her two hands pushing aside the bending leaves. I pulled down the bars of a low rail fence in front of me and hurried to meet her. Her face was flushed.

"Are you not tired?" I whispered.

"Oh, you can speak out now," she said. "I am tired, for it was so rough."

I assisted her to a low rock near the stream, and there we sat down. She took off her hat and fanned herself.

"As soon as I get my breath," she said, "I will tell you about everything."

I was content to wait as long as she pleased, but she soon began :

"I found my uncle in a perfect fury," she said. "He has noticed that the pigeon he put in the balloon is in the habit of coming to my balcony. He suspects me of taking the paper from its wing. And, more than that, he thinks that in some way I have obtained possession of the letter from the person who found the balloon, and that I intend to make some use of it. I tried to quiet him in every way that I could, but it was of no use. Presently he shook his great, long finger at me and said: 'I have made up my mind to wait for the letter until this afternoon's mail comes in and no longer. You can go to the post-office and get me that letter. I want you to go and nobody else. You are the best person to go after it.' I knew very well what he meant by that. He thought that I had the letter and that this would give me a chance to produce it. It seems strange

that he should let me go to the post-office
alone, but his mind must have been greatly
upset, and, besides, I don't believe he thought
there was any need of my going. As soon as
I could I went into the garden to see if you
were still there, and then I put on my hat
and went out. If he saw me he might think
I was going to the post-office, although the
mail does not come in until six o'clock. And
now," her eyes filling with tears as she spoke,
"I cannot go back. I would not dare to go
back to the house without the letter. I think
he is entirely crazy. I have not a thing with
me," she went on to say, "except my gloves
and my hat. I can go to stay with some of
the village people, but they are so near my
uncle's house."

I took one of her hands in both of mine.
"My dear young lady," I said, "you go to
none of them. They would drive you crazy
with their questions. They could not help
you in the least. I will take you to a place
of safety."

"How?" asked she.

I could not instantly formulate my intentions, for the situation had been very suddenly thrust upon me. It was a strange one,

and required consideration. She waited a few moments for me to speak, withdrawing her hand the while.

"I will tell you," she said, "what I thought when I came out here. I thought that I would go back to my school at Stamford, which I left more than a year ago. It is vacation now, but one of the ladies always stays there, and it is the only place I have to go to. I would be afraid to take a train at the village, because someone might see me and interfere with me, but there is a station about two miles below where I would not be likely to meet anyone who knows me. My great difficulty is that I have not any money. I do not mind not having any clothes or things, for Miss Humphreys can give me what I really need, but I must buy my ticket, and I thought perhaps you would lend me the money."

"Oh, that is all right," said I, "you need not trouble yourself about money, but Stamford is a long way from here, and you are not prepared for travel," and as I spoke I looked at her thin white dress. "You can do much better than that. Let me take you to my own home. It is not so far, and my mother

and sister will be glad to welcome and take
care of you. There you can wait until you
hear from your Mrs. Grant, or you can write
to your teacher, or do what you please."

"You are very generous and good," she
said, "but I could not do that. Your mother
does not know me, and, in fact, you do not
know me. What would she think were you
to take me to her? No, I must go to some-
one who knows me—to my school. You may
wonder that I have never written to my
teachers, but there were reasons why I could
not. For a long time they have been very
severe upon my uncle. I know he owes them
money, and he has treated them very rudely.
If I had written to them one of them would
have come here, and there would have been
great trouble. And until this day I never
thought of running away and going to them,
but now I must do it. I can walk to Stillwell, and a train leaves there about ten minutes before six, so there is plenty of time.
As you are so kind as to let me have the
money for my fare I am sure I can easily get
to Stamford."

I saw that her scheme was better than
mine. Her words had called up in my mind

a picture of my mother and sister when I
presented myself before them and requested
them to open their arms to a strange young
woman, very beautiful, but without baggage,
which was a truer picture than the one my
generosity had at first evoked.

"Since you wish it," I said, "you shall go
to Stamford. But you cannot go alone,
and I shall go with you. You will have to
leave this train at the ferry; you must cross to
New York and take another train, and it will
be dark before you get to the end of your
journey. No, do not say a word against it;
you are under my wing, and I shall keep you
there until I give you to your friends, so that
is settled. You say I do not know you, but
I am determined you shall know me, and know
that I am not the kind of a man to let you
go off alone to Stamford at this time of day."

She looked up at me with a smile.

"Are all lawyers as kind-hearted and
thoughtful as you are?" she said.

"It depends on the lawyer," I answered,
and then in a moment added, "and also upon
the client. And now, shall we walk on to
Stillwell?"

She rose without a word, and together we

went out of the woods into the green and
shaded lane.

That walk to Stillwell was a charming one.
The afternoon sky, the summer air, and the
gentle confidences of my companion harmo-
nized like the colors of a tapestry.

But as we approached Stillwell there was
a change in the mood of Miss Rosley. To
the sense of peaceful relief, arising from the
feeling that she was safe and being cared for,
there succeeded a very natural sadness when
she thought that she was thus leaving her
only home and her only relative, and one
who formerly had been so kind to her. As
she spoke of this tears began to roll down
her cheeks. I said everything I could to
comfort and cheer her, and among other
things I suggested that she write to her uncle and let him know where she was going.
He would not disturb her there. She readily
agreed to this, and as there was plenty of
time she sat down on a stone by the road-
side, and with my pencil and on a page from
my notebook she wrote to him, and when we
reached the station I procured an envelope
and mailed it there.

I had a great deal to do to console that

TOGETHER WE WENT OUT OF THE WOODS.

young creature and to keep her from crying during the long and varied journey, but I succeeded fairly well. When we reached New York I found we had an hour and a half to wait. We dined at a restaurant, and leaving her there to finish her dessert I went out and bought her a jacket, for the air was growing very cool. When I brought this to her her eyes sparkled with delight and surprise.

"I believe you are a good fairy," she said. "I was shivering when I came in here, and was just wondering how I could go out into the night air with nothing but this thin dress. And how in the world did you know this would fit me?"

"Do you think my eyes so poor," I asked, "that by this time they are not able to measure you?"

"I did not know," she said, as we went out, "that lawyers had such good eyes."

It was after nine o'clock when we reached the school of the Misses Humphreys, and the elder sister, who, at the time, had the house nearly to herself, was just about to go to her chamber when we arrived. I shall never forget the surprise of that rather more than middle-aged lady when she beheld her former pupil and myself. She took Miss Rosley to her arms, and when the natural agitation of that young lady had subsided I was introduced, and a very brief but direct explanation of her appearance was given.

"I thought you would have to leave him," said Miss Humphreys. "I knew you could not live there, but I never expected you to run away in this fashion. And so this gentleman is your lawyer?" And as she spoke she scanned me very thoroughly through her spectacles.

I soon took my leave, promising to call in the morning for instructions from my client. I went to a hotel, and not until I reached it did I remember that I, as well as Miss Rosley, was unencumbered with baggage.

The next morning I presented myself at Miss Humphreys's school. I had first an interview with the old lady.

"Miss Rosley has told me her story," she said, "balloon and everything, and I must say the affair is entirely different from the circumstances by which we are ordinarily surrounded. She has also explained to me that, although you are apparently too young

a man to have had much law experience, you
are connected with a prominent legal firm
of which I have heard. I hope, sir, that you
will submit this business, with all its details,
to their most careful consideration."

"Of course I shall do that," I said. "I
would not think of acting in such a matter
without the concurrence of the firm."

She smiled.

"I hope you may have their concurrence in
every way," she said. "Miss Rosley has told
me how extraordinarily kind and thoughtful
you have been, and has stated that if you had
known her all your lifetime, instead of part
of a day, your conduct toward her could not
have been more tender or sympathetic. I
inferred, indeed——"

But she did not finish the sentence, for at
this moment Miss Rosley entered the room.
She wore a morning-gown a little too large
for her, but she was quite as lovely as if it
had fitted her. She greeted me warmly.

"I have come," I said, "to take my legal
instructions."

We sat down on a sofa, and Miss Humphreys took a chair at the other end of the
long room. She seemed to think that when

a client was giving instructions to a lawyer
the presence of a witness was necessary.

My instructions were very simple. If possible I was to get an allowance for her, which
would support her, but in no event was I to
do anything which would bring a scandal
upon her uncle or cause his property to be
sold. She had written again to him, telling
him that he need fear nothing from her in
this respect.

"A much too affectionate letter, I should
say," interpolated Miss Humphreys from the
other end of the room.

When our business talk had been concluded Miss Rosley said to me in a rather lower
voice than that in which she had been speaking:

"I can never thank you enough for all you
have done for me, but I shall——"

"Oh, do not speak of that," said I; "wait
until I have done more. You do not know
how glad I am to be able to serve you."

There was an evident restlessness at the
other end of the room, owing, perhaps, to an
inability to catch words spoken in a low
tone and at a considerable distance, and
which seemed to be a hint to speak louder or

to bring the conversation to a close. Under
the circumstances I thought the latter would
be the best course.

"I must go now," I said, "but as soon as
anything definite is done in regard to this
business I will inform you."

"Oh, yes," said she, "I shall be so glad to
have you write and tell me everything."

"Of course I can write," I said, "but it
would be better for me to come to you
wherever you may be and report or consult.
Which would you prefer?" I asked, daring
to speak in quite a low tone. "Shall I write
or come?"

She looked up at me as we stood together,
and said:

"Come."

I reached home that afternoon, and the
next day I went to see Clara. I found her
on fire to know what had happened. As
clearly and concisely as I could I put before
her the event which had occurred since I
saw her. She showed the greatest interest
in every detail of my account. In fact, her
manner indicated a craving for detail. When
I had made what I thought was a good
finish to my story, she said:

"Now then, Tom, there is one thing I particularly want to know; when you were talking to this girl about our willingness to help her, and when you were doing all those things you did, did you always remember to speak to her as one woman to another?"

This question struck me dumb. I did not know what to say. A backward mental glance at the events of the past two days made it still harder to answer. Then up stood Clara, her face somewhat pale.

"Now, be honest, Tom, did you?"

I looked straight into her eyes. "Of course I did not," I said. "I could not do it, and no man who is the right sort of a man could do it. But I spoke to her as a lawyer to his client. You must remember she is my first client."

Clara regarded me for a moment with a smile on her face, a very queer smile. "No, Tom," she said, "she is not your client at all. You know we were to act together in this matter, and as I know nothing of law we could not be her lawyers. There is my cousin Charles, who is a lawyer, and I know he would be very glad to take up this case."

"Your cousin!" I exclaimed with considerable excitement. "You do not suppose that he would speak with her as one woman to another!"

"In this case," said Clara, "it would not matter."

Of course I agreed to give up this, my first case. It was reasonable that I should do so, and I did not argue about it. But it filled my soul with an active jealousy to think of that handsome cousin Charles taking charge of my client's affairs. Against this I argued, but my arguments were of no avail. Clara's cousin was a good lawyer; he was older than I; he had had experience and he had excellent partners, and the matter ended by my giving him a letter of introduction to Miss Rosley, and by putting in his hands her letter to Mrs. Grant, her fortunes and her destinies.

I thought of writing an explanatory note to the young lady, but Clara believed that this was needless. Her cousin could explain everything, and if a note from us should prove necessary she and I could easily write one when the time came to do so. The time for a note from both of us did not arrive, but in about a week after I had parted with Miss

Rosley at the Humphreys's school, and before Clara's cousin had communicated with her, I received a letter from her. That letter I carried unopened in my pocket for three days.

I could not bring myself to believe that it was likely to be a letter which should be read and answered conjointly by Clara and myself, nor could I prevail upon myself that under the circumstances I ought to read it alone. Of course it might be a very simple business note, but whenever I thought of it I seemed to hear a gentle, tender call for sympathy and help. I seemed to see a pair of blue eyes dimmed with tears, and two little hands outstretched toward me. These fancies may have been but stuff and nonsense, but they made such an impression upon me that on the third day I burned that letter without reading it, and I never received another.

Two years have passed since my visit to Wolverton. I am married to Clara, and if I should be lying in a hammock and should see a speck in the blue summer sky I should call her to come to look at it with me.

Clara's cousin Charles is soon to be married to Miss Rosley. He managed her affairs, I am told, as well as could be expected of him, and, although he did not get very much out of the business, he got quite as much as he deserved. I never heard—for I took particular pains not to hear—what Miss Rosley thought of her change of lawyers. Charles is not one of my intimates, and we never have any confidences.

What I have here told was recently recalled by Clara, who came to me with a piece of gray paper in her hand.

"I was looking for some stamps in your desk," she said, "and I found this old postal note for ninety-five cents. I remember it very well. Shall I return it to Grace Rosley, and write on the back of it, 'As one woman to another?' I really think she ought to have it."

I took it from her. "No," said I, "I think I shall keep it; but if you want to put anything on it you can write:

"'A man's a man for a' that.'"

MY WELL AND WHAT CAME OUT
OF IT

MY WELL AND WHAT CAME OUT OF IT

EARLY in my married life I bought a small country estate which my wife and I looked upon as a paradise. After enjoying its delight for a little more than a year our souls were saddened by the discovery that our Eden contained a serpent. This was an insufficient water supply.

It had been a rainy season when we first went there, and for a long time our cisterns gave us full aqueous satisfaction, but early this year a drought had set in and we were obliged to be exceedingly careful of our water.

It was quite natural that the scarcity of water for domestic purposes should affect my wife much more than it did me, and perceiving the discontent which was growing in her mind, I determined to dig a well.

The very next day I began to look for a well-digger. Such an individual was not easy to find, for in the region in which I lived wells had become unfashionable, but I determined to persevere in my search, and in about a week I found a well-digger.

He was a man of somewhat rough exterior, but of an ingratiating turn of mind. It was easy to see that it was his earnest desire to serve me.

"And now then," said he, when we had had a little conversation about terms, "the first thing to do is to find out where there is water. Have you a peach-tree on the place?" We walked to such a tree and he cut therefrom a forked twig.

"I thought," said I, "that divining rods were always of hazel wood."

"A peach twig will do quite as well," said he, and I have since found that he was right. Divining rods of peach will turn and find water quite as well as those of hazel or any other kind of wood.

He took an end of the twig in each hand, and with the point projecting in front of him, he slowly walked along over the grass in my little orchard. Presently the point of the twig seemed to bend itself downward toward the ground.

"There," said he, stopping; "you will find water here."

"I do not want a well here," said I; "this is at the bottom of a hill and my barnyard is at the top; besides, it is too far from the house."

"Very good," said he; "we will try somewhere else."

His rod turned at several other places, but I had objections to all of them. A sanitary engineer had once visited me and he had given me a great deal of advice about drainage, and I knew what to avoid.

We crossed the ridge of the hill into the low ground on the other side. Here were no buildings, nothing which would interfere with the purity of a well. My well-digger walked slowly over the ground with his divining rod. Very soon he exclaimed:

"Here is water!" and picking up a stick, he sharpened one end of it and drove it into the ground. Then he took a string from his pocket, and making a loop in one end he put it over the stick.

"What are you going to do?" I asked.

"I am going to make a circle four feet in diameter," he said. "We have to dig the well as wide as that, you know."

"But I do not want a well there," said I. "It's too close to the wall. I could not build a house over it. It would not do at all."

He stood up and looked at me. "Well, sir," said he, "will you tell me where you would like to have a well?"

"Yes," said I. "I would like to have it over there in the corner of the hedge. It would be near enough to the house; it would have a warm exposure, which will be desirable in winter, and the little house which I intend to build over it would look better there than anywhere else."

He took his divining rod and went to the spot I had indicated. "Is this the place?" he asked, wishing to be sure he had understood me.

"Yes," I replied. He put his twig in position, and in a few seconds it turned in the direction of the ground. Then he drove down a stick, marked out a circle, and the next day he came with two men and a derrick and began to dig my well.

When they had gone down twenty-five feet they found water, and when they had progressed a few feet deeper they began to be afraid of drowning. I thought they ought

to go deeper, but the well-digger said that
they could not dig without first taking out
the water, and that the water came in as fast
as they bailed it out, and he asked me to
put it to myself and tell him how they could
dig it deeper. I put the question to myself
but could find no answer. I also laid the
matter before some specialists, and it was
generally agreed that if water came in as fast
as it was taken out, nothing more could be
desired. The well was, therefore, pronounced
deep enough. It was lined with great tiles,
nearly a yard in diameter, and my well-
digger, after congratulating me on finding
water so easily, bade me good-by and departed
with his men and his derrick.

On the other side of the wall which bounded
my grounds, and near which my well had been
dug, there ran a country lane, leading nowhere in particular, which seemed to be there
for the purpose of allowing people to pass
my house who might otherwise be obliged to
stop.

Along this lane my neighbors would pass,
and often strangers drove by, and as my well
could easily be seen over the low stone wall, its
construction had excited a great deal of inter-

est. Some of the people who drove by were summer folks from the city, and I am sure, from remarks I overheard, that it was thought a very queer thing to dig for water. Of course they must have known that people used to do this in the olden times, even as far back as the time of Jacob and Rebecca, but the expressions of some of their faces indicated that they remembered that this was the nineteenth century.

My neighbors, however, were all rural people, and much more intelligent in regard to water supplies. One of them, Phineas Colwell by name, took a more lively interest in my operations than did anyone else. He was a man of about fifty years of age, who had been a soldier. This fact was kept alive in the minds of his associates by his dress, a part of which was always military. If he did not wear an old fatigue jacket with brass buttons, he wore his blue trousers, or, perhaps, a waistcoat that belonged to his uniform, and if he wore none of these his military hat would appear upon his head. I think he must also have been a sailor, judging from the little gold rings in his ears. But when I first knew him he was a carpenter, who did mason-work when-

ever any of the neighbors had any jobs of the
sort. He also worked in gardens by the day,
and had told me that he understood the care of
horses and was a very good driver. He sometimes worked on farms, especially at harvest-
time, and I know he could paint, for he once
showed me a fence which he said he had
painted. I frequently saw him, because he
always seemed to be either going to his work
or coming from it. In fact, he appeared to
consider actual labor in the light of a bad
habit which he wished to conceal, and which
he was continually endeavoring to reform.

Phineas walked along our lane at least once
a day, and whenever he saw me he told me
something about the well. He did not approve of the place I had selected for it. If
he had been digging a well he would have
put it in a very different place. When I had
talked with him for some time and explained
why I had chosen this spot, he would say
that perhaps I was right, and begin to talk
of something else. But the next time I saw
him he would again assert that if he had
been digging that well he would not have put
it there.

About a quarter of a mile from my house,

at a turn of the lane, lived Mrs. Betty Perch. She was a widow with about twelve children. A few of these were her own, and the others she had inherited from two sisters who had married and died, and whose husbands, having proved their disloyalty by marrying again, were not allowed by the indignant Mrs. Perch to resume possession of their offspring. The casual observer might have supposed the number of these children to be very great—fifteen, or perhaps even twenty—for if he happened to see a group of them on the doorstep, he would see a lot more if he looked into the little garden; and under some cedartrees at the back of the house, there were always some of them on fine days. But perhaps they sought to increase their apparent number and ran from one place to another to be ready to meet observation, as the famous clown, Grimaldi, who used to go through his performances at one London theatre and then dash off in his paint and motley to another, so that a perambulating theatregoing man might imagine that there were two greatest clowns in the world.

When Mrs. Perch had time she sewed for the neighbors, and whether she had time or not she was always ready to supply them with news. From the moment she heard I was going to dig a well she took a vital interest in it. Her own water supply was unsatisfactory, as she depended upon a little spring which sometimes dried up in summer, and should my well turn out to be a good one, she knew I would not object to her sending the children for pails of water on occasions.

"It will be fun for them," she said, "and if your water really is good it will often come in very well for me. Mr. Colwell tells me," she continued, "that you put your well in the wrong place. He is a practical man and knows all about wells, and I do hope that for your sake he may be wrong."

My neighbors were generally pessimists. Country people are proverbially prudent, and pessimism is prudence. We feel safe when we doubt the success of another, because if he should succeed, we can say we were glad we were mistaken, and so step from a position of good judgment to one of generous disposition without feeling that we have changed our plane of merit. But the optimist often gets himself into terrible scrapes, for if he is wrong he cannot say he is glad of it.

But whatever else he may be, a pessimist is depressing, and it was, therefore, a great pleasure to me to have a friend who was an out-and-out optimist. In fact, he might be called a working optimist. He lived about six miles from my house, and had a hobby, which was natural phenomena. He was always on the lookout for that sort of thing, and when he found it he would study its nature and effect. He was a man in the maturity of youth, and if the estate on which he lived had not belonged to his mother, he would have spent much time and money in investigating its natural phenomena. He often drove over to see me, and always told me how glad he would be if he had an opportunity of digging a well.

"I have the wildest desire," he said, "to know what is in the earth under our place, and if it should so happen in the course of time that the limits of earthly existence should be reached by—I mean if the estate should come into my hands—I would go down, down, down until I had found out all that could be discovered. To own a plug of earth four thousand miles long and only know what is on the surface of the upper end of it is unmanly. We might as well be grazing beasts."

He was sorry that I was digging only for water, because water is a very commonplace thing, but he was quite sure I would get it, and when my well was finished he was one of the first to congratulate me.

"But if I had been in your place," said he, "with full right to do as I pleased, I would not have let these men go away. I would have set them to work in some place where there would be no danger of getting water—at least for a long time—and then you would have found out what are the deeper treasures of your land."

Having finished my well, I now set about getting the water into my residence near by. I built a house over the well and put in it a little engine, and by means of a system of pipes, like the arteries and veins of the human body, I proposed to distribute the water to the various desirable points in my house. The engine was the heart which should start the circulation, which should keep it going, which should send throbbing through every pipe, the water, which, if it were not our life, was very necessary to it.

When all was ready we started the engine, and in a very short time we discovered that something was wrong. For fifteen or twenty minutes water flowed into the tank at the top of the house with a sound that was grander in the ears of my wife and myself than the roar of Niagara, and then it stopped. Investigation proved that the flow had stopped because there was no more water in the well.

It is needless to detail the examinations, investigations, and the multitude of counsels and opinions with which our minds were filled for the next few days. It was plain to see that, although this well was fully able to meet the demands of a hand pump or of bailing buckets, the water did not flow into it as fast as it could be pumped out by an engine. Therefore, for the purposes of supplying the circulation of my domestic water system, the well was declared a failure.

My non-success was much talked about in the neighborhood, and we received a great deal of sympathy and condolence. Phineas Colwell was not surprised at the outcome of the affair. He had said that the well had been put in the wrong place. Mrs. Betty was not only surprised, but disgusted.

"It is all very well for you," she said, "who could afford to buy water if it was necessary, but it is very different with the widow and the orphan. If I had not supposed you were going to have a real well, I would have had my spring cleaned out and deepened. I could have had it done in the early summer, but it is of no use now; the spring has dried up."

She told a neighbor that she believed the digging of my well had dried up her spring, and that that was the way of this world, where the widow and the orphan were sure to come out at the little end.

Of course I did not submit to defeat—at least, without a struggle. I had a well, and if anything could be done to make that well supply me with water I was going to do it. I consulted specialists, and, after careful consideration of the matter, they agreed that it would be unadvisable for me to attempt to deepen my present well, as there was reason to suppose there was very little water in the place where I had dug it, and that the very best thing I could do would be to try a driven well. As I had already excavated about thirty feet, that was so much gain to

me, and if I should have a six-inch pipe put
into my present well and then driven down
and down until it came to a place where
there was plenty of water, I would have all I
wanted. How far down the pipe would have
to be driven, of course they did not know,
but they all agreed that if I drove deep
enough I would get all the water I wanted.
This was the only kind of a well, they said,
which one could sink as deep as he pleased
without being interfered with by the water
at the bottom. My wife and I then considered the matter, and ultimately decided that
it would be a waste of the money which we
had already spent upon the engine, the pipes,
and the little house, and, as there was nothing else to be done but to drive a well, we
would have a well driven.

Of course we were both very sorry that
the work must be begun again, but I was especially dissatisfied, for the weather was getting cold, there was already snow upon the
ground, and I was told that work could not
be carried on in winter weather. I lost no
time, however, in making a contract with a
well-driver, who assured me that as soon as
the working season should open, which prob-

ably would be very early in the spring, he would come to my place and begin to drive my well.

The season did open, and so did the pea blossoms, and the pods actually began to fill before I saw that well-driver again. I had had a good deal of correspondence with him in the meantime, urging him to prompt action, but he always had some good reason for delay. (I found out afterward that he was busy fulfilling a contract made before mine in which he promised to drive a well as soon as the season should open.)

At last—it was early in the summer—he came with his derricks, a steam-engine, a trip-hammer, and a lot of men. They took off the roof of my house, removed the engine, and set to work.

For many a long day, and I am sorry to say for many a longer night, that trip-hammer hammered and banged. On the next day, after the night-work began, one of my neighbors came to me to know what they did that for. I told him they were anxious to get through.

"Get through what," said he, "the earth?

If they do that and your six-inch pipe comes out in a Chinaman's back yard he will sue you for damages."

When the pipe had been driven through the soft stratum under the old well, and began to reach firmer ground, the pounding and shaking of the earth became worse and worse. My wife was obliged to leave home with our child.

"If he is to do without both water and sleep," said she, " he cannot long survive." And I agreed with her.

She departed for a pleasant summer resort where her married sister with her child was staying, and from week to week I received very pleasant letters from her, telling me of the charms of the place, and dwelling particularly upon the abundance of cool spring water with which the house was supplied.

While this terrible pounding was going on I heard various reports of its effect upon my neighbors. One of them, an agriculturist, with whom I had always been on the best of terms, came with a clouded brow.

"When I first felt those shakes," he said, "I thought they were the effects of seismic disturbances and I did not mind, but when I found it was your well I thought I ought to come over to speak about it. I do not object to the shaking of my barn, because my man tells me the continual jolting is thrashing out the oats and wheat, but I do not like to have all my apples and pears shaken off my trees. And then," said he, " I have a late brood of chickens, and they cannot walk, because every time they go to make a step they are jolted into the air about a foot. And again, we have had to give up having soup. We like soup, but we do not care to have it spout up like a fountain whenever that hammer comes down."

I was grieved to trouble this friend, and I asked him what I should do. " Do you want me to stop the work on the well?" said I.

" Oh, no," said he, heartily; " go on with the work. You must have water and we will try to stand the bumping. I dare say it is good for dyspepsia, and the cows are getting used to having the grass jammed up against their noses. Go ahead, we can stand it in the daytime, but if you could stop the night-work we would be very glad. Some people may think it a well-spring of pleasure to be bounced out of bed, but I don't."

Mrs. Perch came to me with a face like a squeezed lemon, and asked me if I could lend her five nails. " What sort ? " said I.

"The kind you nail clapboards on with," said she ; " there is one of them been shook entirely off my house by your well. I am in hopes that before the rest are all shook off I shall get in some money that is owing me and can afford to buy nails for myself."

I stopped the night-work, but this was all I could do for these neighbors.

My optimist friend was delighted when he heard of my driven well; he lived so far away that he and his mother were not disturbed by the jarring of the ground. Now he was sure that some of the internal secrets of the earth would be laid bare, and he rode or drove over every day to see what we were getting out of the well. I know that he was afraid we would soon get water, but was too kind-hearted to say so.

One day the pipe refused to go deeper. No matter how hard it was struck, it bounced up again. When some of the substance it had struck was brought up it looked like French chalk, and my optimist eagerly examined it.

" A French-chalk mine," said he, " would

not be a bad thing, but I hoped that you had struck a bed of mineral gutta-percha. That would be a grand find."

But the chalk bed was at last passed and we began again to bring up nothing but common earth.

"I suppose," said my optimist to me one morning, "that you must soon come to water, and if you do I hope it will be hot water."

"Hot water!" I exclaimed, "I do not want that."

"Oh, yes, you would if you had thought about it as much as I have," he replied. "I lay awake for hours last night, thinking what would happen if you struck hot water. In the first place, it would be absolutely pure, because, even if it were possible for germs and bacilli to get down so deep they would be boiled before you got them, and then you could cool that water for drinking. When fresh it would be already heated for cooking and hot baths. And then—just think of it!— you could introduce the hot-water system of heating into your house, and there would be the hot water always ready. But the great thing would be your garden. Think of the refuse hot water circulating in pipes up and down and under all your beds! That garden would bloom in the winter as others do in the summer. At least, you could begin to have lima beans and tomatoes as soon as the frost was out of the air."

I laughed. "It would take a lot of pumping," I said, "to do all that with the hot water."

"Oh, I forgot to say," he cried, with sparkling eyes, "that I do not believe you would ever have any more pumping to do. You have now gone down so far that I am sure whatever you find will force itself up. It will spout high into the air or through all your pipes and run always."

Phineas Colwell was by when this was said, and he must have gone down to Mrs. Betty Perch's house to talk it over with her, for in the afternoon she came to see me.

"I understand," said she, "that you are trying to get hot water out of your well, and that there is likely to be a lot more than you need, so that it will run down by the side of the road. I just want to say that if a stream of hot water comes down past my house some of the children will be bound to get into it and be scalded to death, and I came to say that if that well is going to squirt biling water I'd like to have notice so that I can move, though where a widow with so many orphans is going to move to nobody knows. Mr. Colwell says that if you had got him to tell you where to put that well there would have been no danger of this sort of thing."

The next day the optimist came to me, his face fairly blazing with a new idea. "I rode over on purpose to urge you," he cried, "if you should strike hot water, not to stop there. Go on, and, by George! you may strike fire."

"Heavens!" I cried.

"Oh, quite the opposite," said he, "but do not let us joke. I think that would be the grandest thing of this age. Think of a fire well, with the flames shooting up perhaps a hundred feet into the air!"

I wish Phineas Colwell had not been there. As it was he turned pale and sat down on the wall.

"You look astonished!" exclaimed the optimist, "but listen to me. You have not thought of this thing as I have. If you should strike fire your fortune would be made. By a system of reflectors you could light up the whole country. By means of tiles and pipes this region could be made tropical. You could warm all the houses in the neighborhood with hot air. And then the power you could generate—just think of it! **Heat is** power, the cost of power is the fuel. You could furnish power to all who wanted it; you could fill this region with industries. **My** dear sir, you must excuse my agitation, but if you should strike fire there is no limit to the possibilities of achievement."

"But I want water," said I; "fire would not take the place of that."

"Oh, water is a trifle," said he; "you could have pipes laid from town. It is only about two miles. But fire! Nobody has yet gone down deep enough for that. You have your future in your hands."

As I did not care to connect my future with fire, this idea did not strike me very forcibly, but it struck Phineas Colwell. He did not say anything to me, but after I had gone he went to the well-drivers.

"If you feel them pipes getting hot," he said to them, "I warn you to stop. I have been in countries where there are volcanoes **and I know what they are.** There's enough

of them in this world and there's no need of
making new ones."

In the afternoon a wagoner, who happened
to be passing, brought me a note from Mrs.
Perch, very badly spelled, asking if I would
let one of my men bring her a pail of water,
for she could not think of coming herself or
letting any of the children come near my
place if spouting fires were expected.

The well-driving had gone on and on with
intermissions on account of sickness in the
families of the various workmen, until it had
reached the limit which I had fixed, and we
had not found water in sufficient quantity,
hot or cold, nor had we struck fire, or anything else worth having.

The well-drivers and some specialists were
of the opinion that if I were to go ten, twenty,
or perhaps a hundred feet deeper, I would be
very likely to get all the water I wanted.
But of course they could not tell how deep
they must go, for some wells were over a
thousand feet deep. I shook my head at
this. There seemed to be only one thing
certain about this drilling business, and
that was the expense. I declined to go any
deeper.

"I think," a facetious neighbor said to me, "it would be cheaper for you to buy a lot of Apollinaris water, at wholesale rates, of course, and let your men open so many bottles a day and empty them into your tank. You would find that would pay better in the long run."

Phineas Colwell told me that when he had informed Mrs. Perch that I was going to stop operations, she was in a dreadful state of mind. "After all she had undergone," she said, "it was simply cruel to think of my stopping before I got water, and that after having dried up her spring."

This is what Phineas said she said, but when next I met her she told me that he had declared that if I had put the well where he thought it ought to be, I should have been having all the water I wanted before now.

My optimist was dreadfully cast down when he heard that I would drive no deeper.

"I have been afraid of this," he said. "I have been afraid of it, and if circumstances had so arranged themselves that I should have command of money, I should have been glad to assume the expense of deeper explorations. I have been thinking a great deal about the matter, and I feel quite sure that even if you did not get water or anything else that might prove of value to you, it would be a great advantage to have a pipe sunk into the earth to the depth of, say, one thousand feet."

"What possible advantage could that be?" I asked.

"I will tell you," he said. "You would then have one of the grandest opportunities ever offered to man of constructing a gravity engine. This would be an engine which would be of no expense at all to run. It would need no fuel. Gravity would be the power. It would work a pump splendidly. You could start it when you liked and stop it when you liked."

"Pump!" said I, "what is the good of a pump without water?"

"Oh! of course you would have to have water," he answered; "but, no matter how you get it, you will have to pump it up to your tank so as to make it circulate over your house. Now, my gravity pump would do this beautifully. You see, the pump would be arranged with cog wheels and all that sort of thing, and the power would be supplied by a weight, which would be a cylinder of lead or iron, fastened to a rope and run down inside your pipe. Just think of it! It would run down a thousand feet, and where is there anything worked by weight that has such a fall as that?"

I laughed. "That is all very well," said I; "but how about the power required to wind that weight up again when it got to the bottom? I should have to have an engine to do that."

"Oh, no," said he. "I have planned the thing better than that. You see, the greater the weight the greater the power and the velocity. Now, if you take a solid cylinder of lead about four inches in diameter, so that it would slip easily down your pipe—you might grease it for that matter—and twenty feet in length, it would be an enormous weight, and in slowly descending for about an hour a day —for that would be long enough for your pumping—and going down a thousand feet, it would run your engine for a year. Now then, at the end of the year you could not expect to haul that weight up again. You would have a trigger arrangement which would detach it from the rope when it got to the bottom. Then you would wind up your rope—a man could do that in a short time—and you would attach another cylinder of lead and that would run your engine for another year, minus a few days, because it would only go down 980 feet. The next year you would put on another cylinder and so on. I have not worked out the figures exactly, but I think that in this way your engine would run for thirty years before the pipe became entirely filled with cylinders. That would be probably as long as you would care to have water forced into the house."

"Yes," said I. "I think that is likely." He saw that his scheme did not strike me favorably. Suddenly a light flashed across his face.

"I tell you what you can do with your pipe," he said, "just as it is. You can set up a clock over it which would run for forty years without winding."

I smiled, and he turned sadly away to his horse, but he had not ridden ten yards before he came back and called to me over the wall.

"If the earth at the bottom of your pipe should ever yield to pressure and give way, and if water or gas, or—anything, should be squirted out of it, I beg you will let me know as soon as possible."

I promised to do so.

When the pounding was at an end my wife and child came home. But the season continued dry, and even their presence could not counteract the feeling of aridity which seemed to permeate everything which belonged to us, material or immaterial. We had a great deal of commiseration from our neighbors. I think even Mrs. Betty Perch began to pity us a little, for her spring had begun to trickle again in a small way, and she sent word to me that if we were really in need of water she would be willing to divide with us. Phineas Colwell was sorry for us, of course, but he could not help feeling and saying that if I had consulted him the misfortune would have been prevented.

It was late in the summer when my wife returned, and when she made her first visit of inspection to the grounds and gardens her eyes, of course, fell upon the unfinished well. She was shocked.

"I never saw such a scene of wreckage," she said. "It looks like a Western town after a cyclone. I think the best thing you can do is to have this dreadful litter cleared up, the ground smoothed and raked, the wall mended, and the roof put back on that little house, and then if we can make anybody believe it is an ice-house so much the better."

This was good advice, and I sent for a man to put the vicinity of the well in order and give it the air of neatness which characterizes the rest of our home.

The man who came was named Mr. Barnet. He was a contemplative fellow, with a pipe in his mouth. After having worked at the place for half a day he sent for me and said:

"I will tell you what I would do if I was in your place. I'd put that pump-house in order, and I'd set up the engine, and put the pump down into that thirty-foot well you first dug, and I'd pump water into my house."

I looked at him in amazement.

"There's lots of water in that well," he continued, "and if there's that much now in this drought, you will surely have ever so much more when the weather isn't so dry. I have measured the water and I know."

I could not understand him. It seemed to me that he was talking wildly. He filled his pipe and lighted it and sat upon the wall.

"Now," said he, after he had taken a few puffs, " I'll tell you where the trouble's been with your well. People are always in too big a hurry in this world about all sorts of things as well as wells. I am a well-digger and I know all about them. We know if there is any water in the ground it will always find its way to the deepest hole there is, and we dig a well so as to give it a deep hole to go to in the place where we want it. But you can't expect the water to come to that hole just the very day it's finished. Of course you will get some, because it's right there in the neighborhood, but there is always a lot more that will come if you give it time. It's got to make little channels and passages for itself, and of course it takes time to do that. It's like settling up a new country. Only a few pioneers come at first, and you have to wait for the population to flow in. This being a dry season, and the water in the ground a little sluggish on that account, it was a good while finding out where your well was. If I had happened along when you was talking about a well I think I should have said to you that I knew a proverb which would about fit your case, and that is: 'Let well enough alone.'"

I felt like taking this good man by the hand, but I did not. I only told him to go ahead and do everything that was proper.

The next morning as I was going to the well I saw Phineas Colwell coming down the lane and Mrs. Betty Perch coming up it. I did not wish them to question me, so I stepped behind some bushes. When they met they stopped.

"Upon my word!" exclaimed Mrs. Betty, " if he isn't going to work again on that everlasting well. If he's got so much money he don't know what to do with it, I could tell him that there's people in this world, and not far away either, who would be the better for some of it. It's a sin and a shame, and an abomination. Do you believe, Mr. Colwell, that there is the least chance in the world of his ever getting water enough out of that well to shave himself with?"

"Mrs. Perch," said Phineas, " it ain't no use talking about that well. It ain't no use and it never can be no use, because it's in the wrong place. If he ever pumps water out of that well into his house I'll do——"

"What will you do?" asked Mr. Barnet,

who just then appeared from the recesses of the engine-house.

"I'll do anything on this earth that you choose to name," said Phineas. "I am safe whatever it is."

"Well, then," said Mr. Barnet, knocking the ashes from his pipe preparatory to filling it again, "will you marry Mrs. Perch?"

Phineas laughed. "Yes," he said. "I promised I would do anything, and I'll promise that."

"A slim chance for me," said Mrs. Betty, "even if I'd have you," and she marched on with her nose in the air.

When Mr. Barnet got fairly to work with his derrick, his men, and his buckets, he found that there was a good deal more to do than he had expected. The well-drivers had injured the original well by breaking some of the tiles which lined it, and these had to be taken out and others put in, and in the course of this work other improvements suggested themselves and were made. Several times operations were delayed by sickness in the family of Mr. Barnet, and also in the families of his workmen, but still the work went on in a very fair manner, although much more slowly than had been supposed by any one. But in the course of time—I will not say how much time—the work was finished, the engine was in its place and it pumped water into my house, and every day since then it has pumped all the water we need, pure, cold, and delicious.

Knowing the promise Phineas Colwell had made, and feeling desirous of having everything which concerned my well settled and finished, I went to look for him to remind him of his duty toward Mrs. Perch, but I could not find that naval and military mechanical agriculturist. He had gone away to take a job or a contract—I could not discover which—and he has not since appeared in our neighborhood. Mrs. Perch is very severe on me about this.

"There's plenty of bad things come out of that well," she said, "but I never thought anything bad enough would come out of it to make Mr. Colwell go away and leave me to keep on being a widow with all them orphans."

STEPHEN SKARRIDGE'S
CHRISTMAS

An Archaism

STEPHEN SKARRIDGE'S CHRISTMAS

An Archaism

'TWAS Christmas eve. An adamantine
sky hung dark and heavy over the
white earth. The forests were canescent with
frost, and the great trees bent as if they were
not able to sustain the weight of snow and ice
with which the young winter had loaded them.

In a by-path of the solemn woods there
stood a cottage that would not, perhaps, have
been noticed in the decreasing twilight, had it
not been for a little wisp of smoke that feebly
curled from the chimney, apparently intend-
ing, every minute, to draw up its attenuat-
ed tail, and disappear. Within, around the
hearth whereon the dying embers sent up
that feeble smoke, there gathered the family
of Arthur Tyrrell—himself, his wife, a boy,
and a girl.

'Twas Christmas eve. A damp air rushed

from the recesses of the forest and came, an unbidden guest, into the cottage of the Tyrrells, and it sat on every chair, and lay upon every bed, and held in its chilly embrace every member of the family. All sighed.

"Father," said the boy, "is there no more wood, that I may replenish the fire?"

"No, my son," bitterly replied the father, his face hidden in his hands; "I brought, at noon, the last stick from the wood-pile."

The mother, at these words, wiped a silent tear from her eyes, and drew her children yet nearer the smouldering coals. The father rose and moodily stood by the window, gazing out upon the night. A wind had now arisen, and the dead branches strewed the path that he soon must take to the neighboring town. But he cared not for the danger; his fate and heart were alike hard.

"Mother!" said the little girl, "shall I hang up my stocking to-night? 'Tis Christmas eve."

A Damascus blade could not have cut the mother's heart more keenly than this question.

"No, dear," she faltered.   "You must wear

your stockings—there is no fire—and your feet, uncovered, will freeze."

The little girl sighed, and gazed sadly upon the blackening coals. But she raised her head again and said,

"But, mother dear, if I should sleep with my legs outside the clothes, old Santa Claus might slip in some little things between the stocking and my skin; could he not, dear mother ?"

"Mother is weeping, sister," said the boy, "press her no further."

The father now drew around him his thread-bare coat, put upon his head his well-brushed straw hat, and approached the door.

"Where are you going, this bitter night, dear father?" cried his little son.

"He goes," then said the weeping mother, "to the town. Disturb him not, my son, for he will buy a mackerel for our Christmas din-ner."

"A mackerel!" cried both the children, and their eyes sparkled with joy. The boy sprang to his feet.

"You must not go alone, dear father," he cried. "I will accompany you."

And together they left the cottage.

The streets were crowded with merry faces and well wrapped-up forms. Snow and ice, it is true, lay thick upon the pavements and roofs, but what of that? Bright lights glistened from every window, bright fires warmed and softened the air within the houses, while bright hearts made rosy and happy the countenances of the merry crowd without. In some of the shops great turkeys hung in placid obesity from the bending beams, and enormous bowls of mince-meat sent up delightful fumes, which mingled harmoniously with the scents of the oranges, the apples, and the barrels of sugar and bags of spices. In others, the light from the chandeliers struck upon the polished surface of many a new wheelbarrow, sled, or hobby-horse, or lighted up the placid features of recumbent dolls and the demoniacal countenances of wildly jumping jacks. The crop of marbles and tops was almost more than could be garnered; boxes and barrels of soldiers stood on every side; tin horns hung from every prominence, and boxes of wonders filled the counters; while all the floor was packed with joyous children carrying their little purses. Beyond, there stood the candy-stores—those earthly paradises of the young, where golden gumdrops, rare cream chocolate, variegated mint-stick, and enrapturing mixtures spread their sweetened wealth over all available space.

To these and many other shops and stores and stalls and stands thronged the towns-people, rich and poor. Even the humblest had some money to spend upon this merry Christmas eve. A damsel of the lower orders might here be seen hurrying home with a cheap chicken; here another with a duck; and here the saving father of a family bending under the load of a turkey and a huge basket of good things. Everywhere were cheerful lights and warm hearthstones, bright and gay mansions, cosey and comfortable little tenements, happy hearts, rosy cheeks, and bright eyes. Nobody cared for the snow and ice, while they had so much that was warm and cheering. It was all the better for the holiday—what would Christmas be without snow?

Through these joyous crowds—down the hilarious streets, where the happy boys were shouting, and the merry girls were hurrying in and out of the shops—came a man who was neither joyous, hilarious, merry, nor happy. It was Stephen Skarridge, the landlord of many houses in that town. He wore an overcoat, which, though old, was warm and comfortable, and he had fur around his wrists and his neck. His hat was pushed down tight upon his little head, as though he would shut out all the sounds of merriment which filled the town. Wife and child he had none, and this season of joy to all the Christian world was an annoying and irritating season to his unsympathetic, selfish heart.

"Oh, ho!" he said to himself, as one after another of his tenants, loaded down with baskets and bundles, hurried by, each wishing him a merry Christmas; "oh, ho! there seems to be a great ease in the money market just now. Oh, ho, ho! They all seem as flush as millionnaires. There's nothing like the influence of holiday times to make one open his pockets—ha, ha! It's not yet the first of the month, 'tis true; but it matters not—I'll go and collect my rents to-night, while all this money is afloat—oh, ho! ha, ha!"

Now old Skarridge went from house to house, and threatened with expulsion all who

did not pay their rents that night. Some re-
sisted bravely, for the settlement day had not
yet arrived, and these were served with no-
tices to leave at the earliest legal moment;
others paid up to their dues with many an
angry protest; while some, poor souls, had
no money ready for this unforeseen demand,
and Stephen Skarridge seized whatever he
could find that would satisfy his claim.
Thus many a poor, weeping family saw the
turkey or the fat goose which was to have
graced the Christmas table carried away by
the relentless landlord. The children shed
tears to see their drums and toys depart, and
many a little memento of affection, intended
for a gift upon the morrow, became the property of the hard-hearted Stephen. 'Twas
nearly nine o'clock when Skarridge finished
his nefarious labor. He had converted his
seizures into money, and was returning to
his inhospitable home with more joyous
light in his eyes than had shone there for
many a day, when he saw Arthur Tyrrell
and his son enter the bright main street of
the town.

"Oh, ho!" said Stephen; "has he, too,
come to spend his Christmas money? He,

the poor, miserable, penniless one! I'll follow him."

So behind the unhappy father and his son
went the skulking Skarridge. Past the gro-
cery store and the markets, with their rich
treasures of eatables; past the toy-shops,
where the boy's eyes sparkled with the delight
which disappointment soon washed out with
a tear; past the candy-shops, where the windows were so entrancing that the little fellow
could scarcely look upon them—on, past all
these, to a small shop at the bottom of the
street, where a crowd of the very poorest
people were making their little purchases,
went the father and his son, followed by the
evil-minded Skarridge. When the Tyrrells
went into the shop, the old man concealed
himself outside, behind a friendly pillar, lest
any of these poor people should happen to
be his tenants, and return him the damage
he had just done to them. But he very plainly
saw Arthur Tyrrell go up to the counter and
ask for a mackerel. When one was brought,
costing ten cents, he declined it, but event-
ually purchased a smaller one, the price of
which was eight cents. The two cents which
he received as change were expended for a

modicum of lard, and father and son then left the store and wended their way homeward. The way was long, but the knowledge that they brought, that which would make the next day something more like Christmas than an ordinary day, made their steps lighter and the path less wearisome.

They reached the cottage and opened the door. There, by a rushlight on a table, sat the mother and the little girl, arranging greens wherewith to decorate their humble home. To the mute interrogation of the mother's eyes the father said, with something of the old fervor in his voice:

"Yes, my dear, I have brought it;" and he laid the mackerel on the table. The little girl sprang up to look at it, and the boy stepped back to shut the door; but before he could do so, it was pushed wide open, and Skarridge, who had followed them all the way, entered the cottage. The inmates gazed at him with astonishment; but they did not long remain in ignorance of the meaning of this untimely visit.

"Mr. Tyrrell," said Skarridge, taking out of his pocket a huge memorandum-book, and turning over the pages with a swift and practised hand, "I believe you owe me two months' rent. Let me see—yes, here it is—eighty-seven and a half cents—two months at forty-three and three-quarters cents per month. I should like to have it now, if you please," and he stood with his head on one side, his little eyes gleaming with a yellow maliciousness.

Arthur Tyrrell arose. His wife crept to his side, and the two children ran behind their parents.

"Sir," said Tyrrell, "I have no money—do your worst."

"No money!" cried the hard-hearted Stephen. "That story will not do for me. Everybody seems to have money to-night; and if they have none, it is because they have wilfully spent it. But if you really have none"—and here a ray of hope shot through the hearts of the Tyrrell family—"you must have something that will bring money, and that I shall seize upon. Ah, ha! I will take this!"

And he picked up the Christmas mackerel from the table where Arthur had laid it.

"'Tis very little," said Skarridge, "but it will at least pay me my interest." Wrapping it in the brown paper which lay under it, he thrust it into his capacious pocket, and without another word went out into the night.

Arthur Tyrrell sank into a chair, and covered his face with his hands. His children, dumb with horror and dismay, clung to the rounds of his chair, while his wife, ever faithful in the day of sorrow as in that of joy, put her arm around his neck and whispered in his ear, " Cheer up, dear Arthur, all may yet be well; have courage! He did not take the lard ! "

Swiftly homeward, through the forest, walked the triumphant Skarridge, and he reached his home an hour before midnight. He lived alone, in a handsome house (which he had seized for a debt), an old woman coming every day to prepare his meals and do the little housework that he required. Opening his door with his latch-key, he hurried upstairs, lighted a candle, and seating himself at a large table in a spacious room in the front of the house, he counted over the money he had collected that evening, entered the amount in one of the great folios which lay upon the table, and locked up the cash in a huge safe. Then he took from his pocket the mackerel of the Tyrrell family. He opened it, laid it flat upon the table before him, and divided it by imaginary lines into six parts.

"Here," said he to himself, "are breakfasts for six days—I would it were a week. I like to have things square and even. Had that man bought the ten-cent fish that I saw offered him, there would have been seven portions. Well, perhaps I can make it do, even now—let me see! A little off here—and the same off this—so——"

At this moment something very strange occurred. The mackerel, which had been lying, split open, upon its back, now closed itself, gave two or three long-drawn gasps, and then heaving a sigh of relief, it flapped its tail, rolled its eyes a little, and deliberately wriggling itself over to a pile of ledgers, sat up on its tail, and looked at Skarridge. This astounded individual pushed back his chair and gazed with all his eyes at the strange fish. But he was more astounded yet, when the fish spoke to him. "Would you mind," said the mackerel, making a very wry face, "getting me a glass of water? I feel all of a parch inside."

Skarridge mumbled out some sort of an assent, and hurried to a table near by, where stood a pitcher and a glass, and filling the latter, he brought it to the mackerel. "Will you hold it to my mouth?" said the fish. Stephen complying, the mackerel drank a good half of the water.

"There," it said, "that makes me feel better. I don't mind brine if I can take exercise. But to lie perfectly still in salt water makes one feel wretched. You don't know how hungry I am. Have you any worms convenient?"

"Worms!" cried Stephen, "why, what a question! No, I have no worms."

"Well," said the fish, somewhat petulantly, "you must have some sort of a yard or garden; go and dig me some."

"Dig them!" cried Stephen. "Do you know it's winter, and the ground's frozen—and the worms too, for that matter?"

"I don't care anything for all that," said the mackerel. "Go you and dig some up. Frozen or thawed, it is all one to me now; I could eat them any way."

The manner of the fish was so imperative that Stephen Skarridge did not think of disobeying, but taking a crowbar and a spade from a pile of agricultural implements that lay in one corner of the room (and which had at various times been seized for debts), he lighted a lantern and went down into the little back garden. There he shovelled away the snow, and when he reached the ground he was obliged to use the crowbar vigorously before he could make any impression on the frozen earth. After a half-hour's hard labor, he managed, by most carefully searching through the earth thrown out of the hole he had made, to find five frozen worms. These he considered a sufficient meal for a fish which would scarcely make seven meals for himself, and so he threw down his implements and went into the house, with his lantern, his five frozen worms, and twice as many frozen fingers. When he reached the bottom of the stairs he was certain that he heard the murmur of voices from above. He was terrified. The voices came from the room where all his treasures lay! Could it be thieves?

Extinguishing his lantern and taking off his shoes, he softly crept up the stairs. He had not quite closed the door of the room when he left it, and he could now look through an opening which commanded a view of the whole apartment. And such a sight now met his wide-stretched eyes!

In his chair—his own arm-chair—by the table, there sat a dwarf, whose head, as large as a prize cabbage, was placed upon a body so small as not to be noticeable, and from which depended a pair of little legs appearing like the roots of the before-mentioned vegetable. On the table, busily engaged in dusting a day-book with a pen-wiper, was a fairy, no more than a foot high, and as pretty and graceful as a queen of the ballet viewed from the dress circle. The mackerel still leaned against the pile of ledgers; and—oh horror! —upon a great iron box, in one corner, there sat a giant, whose head, had he stood up, would have reached the lofty ceiling!

A chill, colder than the frosty earth and air outside could cause, ran through the frame of Stephen Skarridge, as he crouched by the crack of the door and looked upon these dreadful visitors, while their conversation, of which he could hear distinctly every word, caused the freezing perspiration to trickle in icy globules down his back.

"He's gone to get me some worms," said the mackerel, "and we might as well settle it all before he comes back. For my part I'm very sure of what I have been saying."

"Oh, yes," said the dwarf; "there can be no doubt about it, at all. I believe it, every word."

"Of course it is so," said the fairy, standing upon the day-book, which was now well dusted; "everybody knows it is."

"It couldn't be otherwise," said the giant, in a voice like thunder among the pines; "we're all agreed upon that."

"They're mighty positive about it, whatever it is," thought the trembling Stephen, who continued to look with all his eyes and to listen with all his ears.

"Well," said the dwarf, leaning back in the chair and twisting his little legs around each other until they looked like a rope's end, "let us arrange matters. For my part, I would like to see all crooked things made straight, just as quickly as possible."

"So would I," said the fairy, sitting down on the day-book, and crossing her dainty satin-covered ankles, from which she stooped to brush a trifle of dust; "I want to see everything nice, and pretty, and just right."

"As for me," said the mackerel, "I'm somewhat divided—in my opinion, I mean—but whatever you all agree upon, will suit me, I'm sure."

"Then," said the giant, rising to his feet, and just escaping a violent contact of his head with the ceiling, "let us get to work, and while we are about it, we'll make a clean sweep of it."

To this the others all gave assent, and the giant, after moving the mackerel to one corner of the table, and requesting the fairy to stand beside the fish, spread all the ledgers, and day-books, and the cash, bill, and memorandum books upon the table, and opened each of them at the first page.

Then the dwarf climbed up on the table and took a pen, and the fairy did the same, and they both set to work, as hard as they could, to take an account of Stephen Skarridge's possessions. As soon as either of them had added up two pages the giant turned over the leaves, and he had to be very busy about it, so active was the dwarf, who had a splendid head for accounts, and who had balanced the same head so long upon his little legs that he had no manner of difficulty in balancing a few ledgers. The fairy, too, ran up and down the columns as if she were dancing a measure in which the only movements were " Forward one ! " and " Backward one ! " and she got over her business nearly as fast as the dwarf. As for the mackerel, he could not add up, but the fairy told him what figures she had to carry to the next column, and he remembered them for her, and thus helped her a great deal. In less than half an hour the giant turned over the last page of the last book, and the dwarf put down on a large sheet of foolscap the sum total of Stephen Skarridge's wealth.

The fairy read out the sum, and the woeful listener at the door was forced to admit to himself that they had got it exactly right.

" Now, then," said the giant, " here is the rent list. Let us make out the schedule." In twenty minutes the giant, the dwarf, and the fairy—the last reading out the names of Stephen's various tenants, the giant stating what amounts he deemed the due of each one, and the dwarf putting down the sums opposite their names — had made out the schedule, and the giant read it over in a voice that admitted of no inattention.

"Hurrah!" said the dwarf. "That's done, and I'm glad," and he stepped lightly from the table to the arm of the chair, and then down to the seat, and jumped to the floor, balancing his head in the most wonderful way, as he performed these agile feats.

"Yes," said the mackerel, "it's all right, though to be sure I'm somewhat divided——"

"Oh! we won't refer to that now," said the giant; "let by-gones be by-gones."

As for the fairy, she did not say a word, but she made a bounce to the top of the day-book which she had dusted, and which now lay closed near the edge of the table, and she danced such a charming little *fantaisie* that everybody gazed at her with delight. The giant stooped and opened his mouth as if he expected her to whirl herself into it when she was done; and the mackerel was actually moved to tears, and tried to wipe his eyes with his fin, but it was not long enough, and so the tears rolled down and hardened into a white crust on the green baize which covered the table. The dwarf was on the floor, and he stood motionless on his little toes, as if he had been a great top dead asleep. Even Stephen, though he was terribly agitated, thought the dance was the most beautiful thing he had ever seen. At length, with a whirl which made her look like a snow-ball on a pivot, she stopped stock-still, standing on one toe, as if she had fallen from the sky and had stuck upright on the day-book.

"Bravo! bravo!" cried the dwarf, and you could hear his little hands clapping beneath his head.

"Hurrah!" cried the giant, and he brought his great palms together with a clap that rattled the window-panes, like the report of a cannon.

"Very nice! very nice, indeed!" said the mackerel. "Though I'm rather di——"

"Oh, no, you're not!" cried the fairy, making a sudden joyful jump at him, and putting her little hand on his somewhat distorted and certainly very ugly mouth. "You're nothing of the kind, and now let's have him in here and make him sign. Do you think he will do it?" said she, turning to the giant. That mighty individual doubled up his great right fist like a trip-hammer, and he opened his great left hand, as hard and solid as an anvil, and he brought the two together with a sounding whang!

"Yes," said he, "I think he will."

"In that case," said the dwarf, "we might as well call him."

"I sent him after some worms," said the mackerel, "but he has not been all this time getting them. I should not wonder at all if he had been listening at the door all the while."

"We'll soon settle that," said the dwarf, walking rapidly across the room, his head rolling from side to side, but still preserving that admirable balance for which it was so justly noted. When he reached the door he pulled it wide open, and there stood poor Stephen Skarridge, trembling from head to foot, with the five frozen worms firmly grasped in his hands.

"Come in!" said the giant, and Stephen walked in slowly and fearfully, bowing as he came, to the several personages in the room.

"Are those my worms?" said the mackerel. "If so, put them in my mouth, one at a time. There! not so fast. They are frozen, sure enough; but do you know that I believe I like them this way the best. I never tasted frozen ones before."

By this time the dwarf had mounted the table, and opening the schedule, stood pointing to an agreement written at the bottom of it, while the fairy had a pen already dipped in the ink, which she held in her hand, as she stood on the other side of the schedule.

"Now, sir!" said the giant, "just take your seat in your chair, take that pen in your hand, and sign your name below that agreement. If you've been listening at the door all this time, as I believe you have, you have heard the contents of the schedule, and therefore need not read it over."

Stephen thought no more of disobeying than he did of challenging the giant to a battle, and he therefore seated himself in his chair, and taking the pen from the fairy, wrote his name at the bottom of the agreement, although he knew that by that act he was signing away half his wealth. When he had written his signature he laid down his pen and looked around to see if anything more was required of him; but just at that moment something seemed to give way in the back of his neck, his head fell forward so as to nearly strike the table, and he awoke!

There was no longer a schedule, a fairy, a dwarf, or a giant. In front of him was the mackerel, split open and lying on its back.

It was all a dream!

For an hour Stephen Skarridge sat at his table, his face buried in his hands. When, at last, his candle gave signs of spluttering out, he arose, and, with a subdued and quiet air, he went to bed.

The next morning was bright, cold, and cheering, and Stephen Skarridge arose very early, went down to the large front room where his treasures were kept, got out his check-book, and for two hours was busily employed in writing. When the old woman who attended to his household affairs arrived at the usual hour, she was surprised at his orders to cook, for his breakfast, the whole of a mackerel which he handed her. When he had finished his meal, at which he ate at least one-half of the fish, he called her up into his room. He then addressed her as follows:

"Margaret, you have been my servant for seventeen years. During that time I have paid you fifty cents per week for your services. I am now convinced that the sum was insufficient; you should have had, at least, two dollars—considering you only had one meal in the house. As you would probably have spent the money as fast as I gave it to you, I shall pay you no interest upon what I have withheld, but here is a check for the unpaid balance—one thousand three hundred and twenty-six dollars. Invest it carefully, and you will find it quite a help to you." Handing the paper to the astounded woman, he took up a large wallet, stuffed with checks, and left the house.

He went down into the lower part of the town, with a countenance full of lively fervor and generous light. When he reached the quarter where his property lay, he spent an hour or two in converse with his tenants, and when he had spoken with the last one, his wallet was nearly empty, and he was followed by a wildly joyful crowd, who would have brought a chair and carried him in triumph through the town, had he not calmly waved them back.

When the concourse of grateful ones had left him, he repaired to the house of Philip Weaver, the butcher, and hired his pony and spring cart. Then he went to Ambrose Smith, the baker (at whose shop he had stopped on his way down-town), and inquired if his orders had been filled. Although it was Christmas morning, Ambrose and his seven assistants were all as busy as bees, but they had not yet been able to fill said orders. In an hour, however, Ambrose came himself to a candy store, where Stephen was treating a crowd of delighted children, and told him all was ready and the cart loaded. At this, Stephen hurried to the baker's shop, mounted the cart, took the reins, and drove rapidly in the direction of the cottage of Arthur Tyrrell. When he reached the place it was nearly one o'clock.

Driving cautiously, as he neared the house, he stopped at a little distance from it, and tied the horse to a tree. Then he stealthily approached a window and looked in.

Arthur Tyrrell sat upon a chair, in the middle of the room, his arms folded and his head bowed upon his breast. On a stool by his left side sat his wife, her tearful eyes raised to his sombre countenance. Before her father stood the little girl, leaning upon his knees and watching the varied expressions that flashed across his face. By his father's right side, his arm resting upon his parent's shoulder, stood the boy, a look of calm resignation far beyond his years lighting up his intelligent face.

'Twas a tableau never to be forgotten!

Able to gaze upon it but a few minutes, Stephen Skarridge pushed open the door and entered the room. His entrance was the signal of consternation. The wife and children fled to the farthest corner of the room, while Arthur Tyrrell arose and sternly confronted the intruder.

"Ha!" said he. "You have soon returned. You think that we can be yet further despoiled. Proceed, take all we have. There is yet this," and he pointed to the two cents' worth of lard, which still lay upon the table.

"No, no," faltered Stephen Skarridge, seizing the hand of Arthur Tyrrell and warmly pressing it. "Keep it! Keep it! 'Tis not for that I came, but to ask your pardon and to beg your acceptance of a Christmas gift. Pardon, for having increased the weight of your poverty, and a gift to celebrate the advent of a happier feeling between us."

Having said this, Stephen paused for a reply. Arthur Tyrrell mused for a moment;
then he cast his eyes upon his wife and his
children, and, in a low but firm voice, he said:

"I pardon and accept!"

"That's right!" cried Skarridge, his whole
being animated by a novel delight; "come
out to the cart, you and your son, and help
me bring in the things, while Mrs. T. and the
girl set the table as quickly as possible. The
cart was now brought up before the door, and
it was rapidly unloaded by willing hands.
From under a half dozen new blankets, which
served to keep the other contents from contact with the frosty air, Stephen first handed
out a fine linen table-cloth, and then a basket
containing a dinner-set of queensware (third
class—seventy-eight pieces with soup-tureen
and pickle-dishes) and a half-dozen knives
and forks (rubber-handled and warranted to
stand hot water). When the cloth had been
spread and the plates and dishes arranged,
Arthur Tyrrell and his son, aided now by the
wife and daughter, brought in the remaining
contents of the cart and placed them on the
table, while, with a bundle of kindling which
he had brought, and the fallen limbs which

lay all about the cottage, Skarridge made a
rousing fire on the hearth.

When the cart was empty and the table
fully spread, it presented indeed a noble
sight.   At one end a great turkey; at the
other, a pair of geese; a duck upon one side
and a pigeon-pie upon the other; cranberries,
potatoes, white and sweet; onions, parsnips,
celery, bread, butter, beets (pickled and but-
tered), pickled cucumbers, and walnuts, and
several kinds of sauces, made up the first
course; while upon a side-table stood mince-
pies, apple-pies, pumpkin-pies, apples, nuts,
almonds, raisins, and a huge pitcher of cider,
for dessert.

It was impossible for the Tyrrell family to
gaze unmoved upon this bounteously spread
table, and after silently clasping each other
for a moment, they sat down, with joyful,
thankful hearts, to a meal far better than
they had seen for years.   At their earnest
solicitation Mr. Skarridge joined them.

When the meal was over, and there was
little left but empty dishes, they all arose,
and Skarridge prepared to take his leave.

" But before I go," said he, " I would leave
with you a further memento of my good feel-

ing and friendship. You know my Hillsdale farm, in the next township?"

"Oh, yes!" cried Arthur Tyrrell; "is it possible that you will give me a position there?"

"I make you a present of the whole farm," said Skarridge. "There are two hundred and forty-two acres, sixty of which are in timber; large mansion-house, two good barns, and cow and chicken houses; a well, covered in; an orchard of young fruit-trees, and a stream of water flowing through the place. The estate is well stocked with blooded cattle, horses, etc., and all necessary farming utensils. Possession immediate."

Without waiting for the dumfounded Tyrrell to speak, Skarridge turned quickly to his wife, and said: "Here, madam, is my Christmas-gift to you. In this package you will find shares of the New York Central and Hudson (sixes, of 'eighty-three), of the Fort Wayne (guaranteed), and of the St. Paul's (preferred); also bonds of the Delaware, Lackawanna, and Western (second mortgage), and of the Michigan Seven Per Cent. War Loan. In all these amount to nine thousand and eighty-two dollars; but to preclude the necessity of sell-ing at a sacrifice, for immediate wants, I have taken the liberty of placing in the package one thousand dollars in greenbacks. And now, dear friends, adieu!"

But the grateful family could not allow this noble man to leave them thus. Arthur Tyrrell seized his hand and pressed it to his bosom, and then, as if overcome with emotion, Mrs. Tyrrell fell upon her benefactor's neck, while the children gratefully grasped the skirts of his coat. With one arm around the neck of the still young, once beautiful, and now fast improving Mrs. Tyrrell, Stephen Skarridge stood for a few minutes, haunted by memories of the past. Then he spoke:

"Once," said he, his voice trembling the while, "once—I, too—loved such a one. But it is all over now—and the grass waves over her grave. Farewell, farewell dear friends!" and dashing away a tear, he tore himself from the fervent family, and swiftly left the house.

Springing into the cart, he drove rapidly into the town—a happy man! . . .

Did you ever before read a story like this?

MY UNWILLING NEIGHBOR

MY UNWILLING NEIGHBOR

I WAS about twenty-five years old when I began life as the owner of a vineyard in western Virginia. I bought a large tract of land, the greater part of which lay upon the sloping side of one of the foot-hills of the Blue Ridge, the exposure being that most favorable to the growth of the vine. I am an enthusiastic lover of the country and of country life, and believed that I should derive more pleasure as well as profit from the culture of my far-stretching vineyard than I would from ordinary farm operations.

I built myself a good house of moderate size upon a little plateau on the higher part of my estate. Sitting in my porch, smoking my pipe after the labors of the day, I could look down over my vineyard into a beautiful valley, with here and there a little curling smoke arising from some of the few dwellings which were scattered about among the groves and spreading fields, and above this beauty I could imagine all my hillside clothed in green and purple.

My family consisted of myself alone. It is true that I expected some day that there would be others in my house besides myself, but I was not ready for that yet.

During the summer I found it very pleasant to live by myself. It was a novelty, and I could arrange and manage everything in my own fashion, which was a pleasure I had not enjoyed when I lived in my father's house; but when winter came I found it very lonely. Even my servants lived in a cabin at some little distance, and there were many dark and stormy evenings when the company even of a bore would have been welcome to me. Sometimes I walked over to the town and visited my friends there, but this was not feasible on stormy nights, and the winter seemed to me a very long one.

But spring came, out-door operations began, and for a few weeks I felt again that I was all-sufficient for my own pleasure and comfort. Then came a change. One of those seasons of bad and stormy weather which so frequently follow an early spring settled down upon my spirits and my hillside. It rained, it was cold, fierce winds blew, and I became more anxious for somebody to talk to than I had been at any time during the winter.

One night, when a very bad storm was raging, I went to bed early, and as I lay awake I revolved in my mind a scheme of which I had frequently thought before. I would build a neat little house on my grounds, not very far away from my house, but not too near, and I would ask Jack Brandiger to come there and live. Jack was a friend of mine who was reading law in the town, and it seemed to me that it would be much more pleasant, and even more profitable, to read law on a pretty hillside overlooking a charming valley, with woods and mountains behind and above him, where he could ramble to his heart's content.

I had thought of asking Jack to come and live with me, but this idea I soon dismissed. I am a very particular person, and Jack was not; he left his pipes about in all sorts of places—sometimes when they were still lighted. When he came to see me he was quite as likely to put his hat over the inkstand as to put it anywhere else. But if

Jack lived at a little distance, and we could go backwards and forwards to see each other whenever we pleased, that would be quite another thing. He could do as he pleased in his own house, and I could do as I pleased in mine, and we might have many pleasant evenings together. This was a cheering idea, and I was planning how we might arrange with the negro woman who managed my household affairs to attend also to those of Jack when I fell asleep.

I did not sleep long before I was awakened by the increased violence of the storm. My house shook with the fury of the wind; the rain seemed to be pouring on its roof and northern side as if there were a waterfall above us; and every now and then I could hear a shower of hailstones rattling against the shutters. My bedroom was one of the rooms on the lower floor, and even there I could hear the pounding of the deluge and the hailstones upon the roof.

All this was very doleful, and had a tendency to depress the spirits of a man, awake and alone in a good-sized house; but I shook off this depression. It was not agreeable to be up here by myself in such a terrible storm,

but there was nothing to be afraid of, as my
house was new and very strongly built, being constructed of logs, weather-boarded outside and ceiled within. It would require a
hurricane to blow off the roof, and I believed
my shutters to be hail-proof; so, as there was
no reason to stay awake, I turned over and
went to sleep.

I do not know how long it was before I
was awakened again, this time not by the
noise of the storm, but by a curious movement of my bedstead. I had once felt the
slight shock of an earthquake, and it seemed
to me that this must be something of the
kind; certainly my bed moved under me. I
sat up; the room was pitchy dark. In a moment I felt another movement, but this time
it did not seem to me to resemble an earthquake shock; such motion, I think, is generally in horizontal directions, while that
which I felt was more like the movement of
a ship upon the water. The storm was at
its height, the wind raged and roared, and
the rain seemed to be pouring down as heavily as ever.

I was about to get up and light the lamp
for even the faintest candle flame would be

some sort of company at such a grewsome moment, when my bedstead gave another movement, more shiplike than before. It actually lurched forward as if it were descending into the trough of the sea, but unlike a ship, it did not rise again, but remained in such a slanting position that I began to slide down toward the foot. I believe that if it had not been a bedstead provided with a foot-board, I should have slipped out upon the floor.

I did not jump out of bed; I did not do anything. I was trying to think, to understand the situation, to find out whether I was asleep or awake, when I became aware of noises in the room and all over the house, which even through the din of the storm made themselves noticed by their peculiarity. Tables, chairs, everything in the room, seemed to be grating and grinding on the floor, and in a moment there was a crash. I knew what that was; it was my lamp, which had slipped off the table. Any doubt on that point would have been dispelled by the smell of kerosene, which filled the air of the room.

The motion of the bed, which I now believe must have been the motion of the whole house, still continued; but the grating noises in the room gradually ceased, from which I inferred that the furniture had brought up against the front wall of the room.

It now was impossible for me to get up and strike a light, for to do so, with kerosene oil all over the floor and its vapor diffused through the room, would probably result in setting the house on fire; so I must stay in darkness and wait. I do not think I was very much frightened—I was so astonished that there was no room in my mind for fear. In fact, all my mental energies were occupied in trying to find out what had happened. It required, however, only a few more minutes of reflection and a few more minutes of the grating, bumping, trembling of my house to enable me to make up my mind what was happening: my house was sliding downhill!

The wind must have blown the building from its foundations, and, upon the slippery surface of the hillside, probably lashed into liquid mud by the pouring rain, it was making its way down toward the valley! In a flash my mind's eye ran over the whole surface of the country beneath me as far as I knew it. I was almost positive that there

was no precipice, no terrible chasm into
which my house might fall. There was nothing but sloping hillside, and beneath that a
wide stretch of fields.

Now there was a new and sudden noise of
heavy objects falling upon the roof, and I
knew what that meant: my chimney had
been wrenched from its foundations, and the
upper part of it had now toppled over. I
could hear, through the storm, the bricks
banging and sliding upon the slanting roof.
Continuous sounds of cracking and snapping
came to me through the closed front windows,
and these were caused I supposed by the de-
struction of the stakes of my vines, as the
heavy house moved over them.

Of course, when I thoroughly understood
the state of the case, my first impulse was to
spring out of bed, and, as quickly as possible,
to get out of that thumping and sliding house;
but I restrained myself. The floor might be
covered with broken glass, I might not be able
to find my clothes in the darkness and in the
jumble of furniture at the end of the room,
and even if I could dress myself, it would be
folly to jump out in the midst of that raging
storm into a probable mass of wreckage

which I could not see; it would be far better to remain dry and warm under my roof. There was no reason whatever to suppose that the house would go to pieces, or that it would turn over; it must stop some time or other; and, until it did so, I would be safer in my bed than anywhere else. Therefore in my bed I stayed.

Sitting upright, with my feet pressed against the foot-board, I listened and felt. The noises of the storm, and the cracking and the snapping and grinding before me and under me, still continued, although I sometimes thought that the wind was moderating a little, and that the strange motion was becoming more regular. I believed the house was moving faster than when it first began its strange career, but that it was sliding over a smooth surface. Now I noticed a succession of loud cracks and snaps at the front of the house, and, from the character of the sounds, I concluded that my little front porch, which had been acting as a cutwater at the bow of my shiplike house, had yielded at last to the rough contact with the ground, and would probably soon be torn away. This did not disturb me, for the house must still be firm.

It was not long before I perceived that the slanting of my bed was becoming less and less, and also I was quite sure that the house was moving more slowly. Then the crackings and snappings before my front wall ceased altogether. The bed resumed its ordinary horizontal position, and, although I did not know at what moment the house had ceased sliding and had come to a standstill, I was sure that it had done so. It was now resting upon a level surface. The room was still perfectly dark, and the storm continued. It was useless for me to get up until daylight came—I could not see what had happened—so I lay back upon my pillow and tried to imagine upon what level portion of my farm I had stranded. While doing this I fell asleep.

When I woke, a little light was stealing into the room through the blinds of my shutters. I quickly slipped out of bed, opened a window, and looked out. Day was just breaking, the rain and wind had ceased, and I could discern objects ; but it seemed as if I needed some light in my brain to enable me to comprehend what I saw. My eyes fell upon nothing familiar.

I did not stop to investigate, however, from my window. I found my clothes huddled together with the furniture at the front end of the room, and as soon as I was dressed I went into the hall and then to my front door. I quickly jerked this open, and was about to step outside when, suddenly, I stopped. I was positive that my front porch had been destroyed; but there I saw a porch, a little lower than mine and a great deal wider, and on the other side of it, not more than eight feet from me, was a window—the window of a house; and on the other side of the window was a face—the face of a young girl! As I stood staring in blank amazement at the house which presented itself at my front door, the face at the window disappeared, and I was left to contemplate the scene by myself. I ran to my back door and threw it open. There I saw, stretching up the fields and far up the hillside, the wide path which my house had made as it came down from its elevated position to the valley beneath, where it had ended its onward career by stopping up against another house. As I looked from the back porch I saw that the ground still continued to slope, so that if my house had

not found in its path another building, it
would probably have proceeded somewhat
farther on its course. It was lighter, and I
saw bushes and fences and outbuildings—I
was in a back yard.

Almost breathless with amazement and
consternation, I ran again to the front door.
When I reached it I found a young woman
standing on the porch of the house before
me. I was about to say something—I know
not what—when she put her finger on her lips
and stepped forward.

"Please don't speak loudly," she said. "I
am afraid it will frighten mother; she is
asleep yet. I suppose you and your house
have been sliding down hill?"

"That is what has happened," said I; "but
I cannot understand it; it seems to me the
most amazing thing that ever took place on
the face of the earth."

"It is very queer," said she; "but hurri-
canes do blow away houses, and that must
have been a hurricane we had last night, for
the wind was strong enough to loosen any
house. I have often wondered if that house
would ever slide downhill."

"My house?"

"Yes," she said. "Soon after it was built I began to think what a nice clean sweep it could make from the place where it seemed to be stuck to the side of the mountain, right down here into the valley."

I could not talk with a girl like this; at least I could not meet her on her own conversational grounds. I was so agitated myself that it seemed unnatural that any one to whom I should speak should not also be agitated.

"Who are you?" I asked, rather brusquely; "at least, to whom does this house belong?"

"This is my mother's house," said she. "My mother is Mrs. Carson. We happen just now to be living here by ourselves, so I cannot call on any man to help you do anything. My brother has always lived with us, but last week he went away."

"You don't seem to be a bit astonished at what has happened," said I.

She was rather a pretty girl; of a cheerful disposition, I should say, for several times she had smiled as she spoke.

"Oh, I am astonished," she answered; "or at least I was, but I have had time enough

to get over some of it. It was at least an
hour ago when I was awakened by hearing
something crack in the yard. I went to a
window and looked out, and could just barely
see that something like a big building had
grown up during the night. Then I watched
it, and watched it, until I made out it was a
whole house; and after that it was not long
before I guessed what had happened. It
seemed a simpler thing to me, you know,
than it did to you, because I had often thought
about it, and probably you never had."

"You are right there," said I, earnestly.
"It would have been impossible for me to
imagine such a thing."

"At first I thought there was nobody in the
house," said she; "but when I heard some-
one moving about, I came down to tell whoever had arrived not to make a noise. I
see," she added, with another of her smiles,
"that you think I am a very strange person
not to be more flurried by what has happened; but really I cannot think of anything
else just now except what mother will say
and do when she comes down and finds you
and your house here at the back door. I am
very sure she will not like it."

"Like it!" I exclaimed. "Who on earth could like it?"

"Please speak more gently," she said. "Mother is always a little irritable when her night's rest has been broken, and I would not like to have her wakened up suddenly now. But really, Mr. Warren, I haven't the least idea in the world how she will take this thing. I must go in and be with her when she wakes, so that I can explain just what has happened."

"One moment," I said. "You know my name."

"Of course I know your name," she answered. "Could that house be up there on the hillside for more than a year without my knowing who lived in it?" With this, she went indoors.

I could not help smiling when I thought of the young lady regretting that there was no man in the house who might help me do something. What could anybody do in a case like this? I turned and went into my house. I entered the various rooms on the lower floor, and saw no signs of any particular damage except that everything movable in each room was jumbled together against the front wall. But when I looked out of the back door I found that the porch there was a good deal wrecked, which I had not noticed before.

I went upstairs, and found everything very much as it was below. Nothing seemed to have been injured except the chimney and the porches. I thanked my stars that I had used hard wood instead of mortar for the ceilings of my rooms.

I was about to go into my bedroom, when I heard a woman scream, and of course I hurried to the front. There on the back porch of her house stood Mrs. Carson. She was a woman of middle age, and, as I glanced at her, I saw where her daughter got her good looks. But the placidity and cheerfulness of the younger face were entirely wanting in the mother. Her eyes sparkled, her cheeks were red, her mouth was partly opened, and it seemed to me that I could almost see that her breath was hot.

"Is this your house?" she cried, the moment her eyes fell upon me; "and what is it doing here?"

I did not immediately answer. I looked at the angry woman, and behind her I saw, through the open door, the daughter crossing the hallway. It was plain that she had decided to let me have it out with her mother without interference. As briefly and as clearly as I could, I explained what had happened.

"What is all that to me?" she screamed. "It doesn't matter to me how your house got here. There have been storms ever since the beginning of the world, and I never heard of any of them taking a house into a person's back yard. You ought not to have built your house where any such thing could happen. But all this is nothing to me. I don't understand, now, how your house did get here, and I don't want to understand it. All I want is for you to take it away."

"I will do that, madam, just as soon as I can. You may be very sure I will do that. But——"

"Can you do it now?" she asked. "Can you do it to-day? I don't want a minute lost. I have not been outside to see what damage has been done, but the first thing to do is to take your house away."

"I am going to the town now, madam, to summon assistance."

Mrs. Carson made no answer, but she turned and walked to the end of her porch. There she suddenly gave a scream, which quickly brought her daughter from the house. "Kitty! Kitty!" cried her mother. "Do you know what he has done? He has gone right over my round flower garden; his house is sitting on it this minute!"

"But he could not help it, mother," said Kitty.

"Help it!" exclaimed Mrs. Carson. "I didn't expect him to help it; what I want—" Suddenly she stopped. Her eyes flashed brighter, her mouth opened wider, and she became more and more excited as she noticed the absence of sheds, fences, or vegetable beds, which had found themselves in the course of my all-destroying dwelling.

It was now well on in the morning, and some of the neighbors had become aware of the strange disaster which had happened to me, although if they had heard the news from Mrs. Carson they might have supposed that it was a disaster which had happened only to her. As they gazed at the two houses so closely jammed together, all of them wondered, some of them even laughed, but not one offered a suggestion which afforded satisfaction to Mrs. Carson or myself. The general opinion was that, now my house was there, it would have to stay there, for there were not enough horses in the State to pull it back up that mountain-side. To be sure, it might possibly be drawn off sidewise; but whether it was moved one way or the other, a lot of Mrs. Carson's trees would have to be cut down to let it pass.

"Which shall never happen!" cried that good lady. "If nothing else can be done, it must be taken apart and hauled off in carts; but, no matter how it is managed, it must be moved, and that immediately."

Miss Carson now prevailed upon her mother to go into the house, and I stayed and talked to the men and a few women who had gathered outside.

When they had said all they had to say, and seen all there was to see, these people went home to their breakfasts. I entered my house, but not by the front door, for to do that I would have been obliged to trespass upon Mrs. Carson's back porch. I got my hat, and was about to start for the town, when I heard my name called. Turning into the hall, I saw Miss Carson, who was standing at my front door.

"Mr. Warren," said she, "you haven't any way of getting breakfast, have you?"

"Oh, no," said I. "My servants are up there in their cabin, and I suppose they are too much scared to come down. But I am going to town to see what can be done about my house, and will get my breakfast there."

"It's a long way to go without anything to eat," she said, "and we can give you some breakfast. But I want to ask you something. I am in a good deal of perplexity; our two servants are out at the front of the house, but they positively refuse to come in. They are afraid that your house may begin sliding again and crush them all, so I shall have to get breakfast. But what bothers me is trying to find our well. I have been outside, and can see no signs of it."

"Where was your well?" I gasped.

"It ought to be somewhere near the back of your house," she said. "May I go through your hall and look out?"

"Of course you may," I cried, and I preceded her to my back door.

"Now, it seems to me," she said, after sur-

I BEGAN TO SEARCH FOR THE WELL.

veying the scene of desolation immediately before, and looking from side to side, toward objects which had remained untouched, "that your house has passed directly over our well, and must have carried away the little shed and the pump and everything above ground. I should not wonder a bit," she continued slowly, "if it is under your porch."

I jumped to the ground, for the steps were shattered, and began to search for the well, and it was not long before I discovered its round dark opening, which was, as Miss Carson had imagined, under one end of my porch.

"What can we do?" she asked. "We can't have breakfast or get along at all without water." It was a terribly depressing thing to me to think that I, or rather my house, had given these people so much trouble; but I speedily assured Miss Carson that if she could find a bucket and a rope, which I could lower into the well, I would provide her with water.

She went into her house to see what she could find, and I tore away the broken planks of the porch, so that I could get to the well; and then, when she came with a tin pail and a clothes-line, I went to work to haul up water and carry it to her back door.

"I don't want mother to find out what has happened to the well," she said; "for she has enough on her mind already."

Mrs. Carson was a woman with some good points in her character. After a time she called to me herself, and told me to come in to breakfast; but during the meal she talked very earnestly to me about the amazing trespass I had committed and about the means which should be taken to repair the damages my house had done to her property. I was as optimistic as I could be, and the young lady spoke very cheerfully and hopefully about the affair, so that we were beginning to get along somewhat pleasantly, when, suddenly, Mrs. Carson sprang to her feet. "Heavens and earth!" she cried, "this house is moving!"

She was not mistaken. I had felt beneath my feet a sudden sharp shock—not severe, but unmistakable. I remembered that both houses stood upon slightly sloping ground; my blood turned cold, my heart stood still— even Miss Carson was pale!

When we had rushed out-of-doors to see

what had happened, or what was going to happen, I soon found that we had been needlessly frightened. Some of the broken timbers on which my house had been partially resting had given away, and the front part of the building had slightly descended, jarring as it did so the other house against which it rested. I endeavored to prove to Mrs. Carson that the result was encouraging rather than otherwise, for my house was now more firmly settled than it had been; but she did not value the opinion of a man who did not know enough to put his house in a place where it would be likely to stay, and she could eat no more breakfast, and was even afraid to stay under her own roof until experienced mechanics had been summoned to look into the state of affairs.

I hurried away to the town, and it was not long before several carpenters and masons were on the spot. After a thorough examination, they assured Mrs. Carson that there was no danger, that my house would do no further damage to her premises; but, to make things certain, they would bring some heavy beams and brace the front of my house against her cellar wall. When that should be done it would be impossible for it to move any farther.

"But I don't want it braced!" cried Mrs. Carson. "I want it taken away; I want it out of my back yard!"

The master carpenter was a man of imagination and expedients. "That is quite another thing, ma'am," said he. "We'll fix this gentleman's house so that you needn't be afraid of it; and then when the time comes to move it, there's several ways of doing that. We might rig up a powerful windlass at the top of the hill, and perhaps get a steam-engine to turn it, and we could fasten cables to the house and haul her back to where she belongs."

"And can you take your oaths," cried Mrs. Carson, "that those ropes won't break, and when that house gets half way up the hill, it won't come sliding down ten times faster than it did, and crash into me and mine and everything I own on earth? No, sir! I'll have no house hauled up a hill back of me!"

"Of course," said the carpenter, "it would be a great deal easier to move it on this ground, which is almost level——"

"And cut down my trees to do it! No, sir!"

"Well, then," said he, "there is no way to do but to take it apart and haul it off."

"Which would make an awful time at the back of my house while you were doing it!" exclaimed Mrs. Carson.

I now put in a word. "There's only one thing to do that I can see!" I exclaimed. "I will sell it to a match factory. It is almost all wood, and it can be cut up in sections about two inches thick, and then split into matches."

Kitty smiled. "I should like to see them," she said, "taking away the little sticks in wheelbarrows!"

"There is no need of trifling on the subject," said Mrs. Carson. "I have had a great deal to bear, and I must bear it no longer than is necessary. I have just found out that in order to get water out of my own well, I must go to the back porch of a stranger. Such things cannot be endured. If my son George were here, he would tell me what I ought to do. I shall write to him, and see what he advises. I do not mind waiting a little bit, now that I know that you can fix

Mr. Warren's house so that it won't move any farther."

Thus the matter was left. My house was braced that afternoon, and toward evening I started to go to a hotel in the town to spend the night.

"No, sir!" said Mrs. Carson. "Do you suppose that I am going to stay here all night with a great empty house jammed up against me, and everybody knowing that it is empty? It will be the same as having thieves in my own house to have them in yours. You have come down here in your property, and you can stay in it and take care of it!"

"I don't object to that in the least," I said. "My two women are here, and I can tell them to attend to my meals. I haven't any chimney, but I suppose they can make a fire some way or other."

"No, sir!" said Mrs. Carson. "I am not going to have any strange servants on my place. I have just been able to prevail upon my own women to go into the house, and I don't want any more trouble; I have had enough already!"

"But, my dear madam," said I, "you don't

want me to go to the town, and you won't allow me to have any cooking done here; what
am I to do?"

"Well," she said, "you can eat with us. It
may be two or three days before I can hear
from my son George, and in the meantime
you can lodge in your own house and I will
take you to board. That is the best way I
can see of managing the thing; but I am very
sure I am not going to be left here alone in
the dreadful predicament in which you have
put me."

We had scarcely finished supper, when
Jack Brandiger came to see me. He laughed
a good deal about my sudden change of base,
but thought, on the whole, my house had
made a very successful move; it must be more
pleasant in the valley than up on that windy
hill. Jack was very much interested in everything, and when Mrs. Carson and her daughter appeared, as we were walking about
viewing the scene, I felt myself obliged to
introduce him.

"I like those ladies," said he to me afterward. "I think you have chosen very agreeable neighbors."

"How do you know you like them?" said

I.   "You had scarcely anything to say to Mrs. Carson."

"No, to be sure," said he; "but I expect I should like her. By the way, do you know how you used to talk to me about coming and living somewhere near you? How would you like me to take one of your rooms now?   I might cheer you up."

"No," said I, firmly. "That cannot be done. As things are now, I have as much as I can do to get along here by myself."

Mrs. Carson did not hear from her son for nearly a week, and then he wrote that he found it almost impossible to give her any advice. He thought it was a very queer state of affairs ; he had never heard of anything like it; but he would try and arrange business so that he could come home in a week or two and look into matters.

As I was thus compelled to force myself upon the close neighborhood of Mrs. Carson and her daughter, I endeavored to make things as pleasant as possible. I brought some of my men down out of the vineyard and set them to repairing fences, putting the garden in order, and doing all that I could to remedy the doleful condition of things which I had unwillingly brought into the back yard of this quiet family. I rigged up a pump on my back porch by which the water of the well could be conveniently obtained, and in every way endeavored to repair damages.

But Mrs. Carson never ceased to talk about the unparalleled disaster which had come upon her, and she must have had a great deal of correspondence with her son George, because she gave me frequent messages from him. He could not come on to look into the state of affairs, but he seemed to be giving it a great deal of thought and attention.

Spring weather had come again, and it was very pleasant to help the Carson ladies get their flower-garden in order — at least as much as was left of it, for my house was resting upon some of the most important beds. As I was obliged to give up all present idea of doing anything in the way of getting my residence out of a place where it had no business to be, because Mrs. Carson would not consent to any plan which had been suggested, I felt that I was offering some little compensation in beautifying what seemed to be, at that time, my own grounds.

My labors in regard to vines, bushes, and all that sort of thing, were generally carried on under direction of Mrs. Carson or her daughter, and as the elderly lady was a very busy housewife, the horticultural work was generally left to Miss Kitty and me.

I liked Miss Kitty; she was a cheerful, whole-souled person, and I sometimes thought that she was not so unwilling to have me for a neighbor as the rest of the family seemed to be; for if I were to judge the disposition of her brother George from what her mother told me about his letters, both he and Mrs. Carson must be making a great many plans to get me off the premises.

Nearly a month had now passed since my house and I made that remarkable morning call upon Mrs. Carson. I was becoming accustomed to my present mode of living, and, so far as I was concerned, it satisfied me very well; I certainly lived a great deal better than when I was depending upon my old negro cook. Miss Kitty seemed to be satisfied with things as they were, and so, in some respects, did her mother; but the latter never ceased to give me extracts from some of her son George's letters, and this was always annoying and worrying to me. Evidently he was not pleased with me as such a close neighbor to his mother; and it was astonishing how many expedients he proposed in order to rid her of my undesirable proximity.

"My son George," said Mrs. Carson, one morning, "has been writing to me about jackscrews; he says that the greatest improvements have been made in jackscrews."

"What do you do with them, mother?" asked Miss Kitty.

"You lift houses with them," said she. "He says that in large cities they lift whole blocks of houses with them and build stories underneath. He thinks that we can get rid of our trouble here if we use jackscrews."

"But how does he propose to use them?" I asked.

"Oh, he has a good many plans," answered Mrs. Carson. "He said that he should not wonder if jackscrews could be made large enough to lift your house entirely over mine and set it out in the road, where it could be carried away without interfering with anything, except, of course, vehicles which might be coming along. But he has another plan;

that is, to lift my house up and carry it out into the field on the other side of the road, and then your house might be carried along right over the cellar until it got to the road. In that way, he says, the bushes and trees would not have to be interfered with."

"I think brother George is cracked!" said Kitty.

All this sort of thing worried me very much. My mind was eminently disposed toward peace and tranquillity, but who could be peaceful and tranquil with a prospective jackscrew under the very base of his comfort and happiness? In fact, my house had never been such a happy home as it was at that time; the fact of its unwarranted position upon other people's grounds had ceased to trouble me.

But the coming son George, with his jack-screws, did trouble me very much, and that afternoon I deliberately went into Mrs. Carson's house to look for Kitty. I knew her mother was not at home, for I had seen her go out. When Kitty appeared I asked her to come out on her back porch. "Have you thought of any new plan of moving it?" she said, with a smile, as we sat down.

"No," said I, earnestly; "I have not, and I don't want to think of any plan of moving it. I am tired of seeing it here, I am tired of thinking about moving it away, and I am tired of hearing people talk about moving it. I have not any right to be here, and I am never allowed to forget it. What I want to do is to go entirely away, and leave everything behind me—except one thing."

"And what is that?" asked Kitty.

"You," I answered.

She turned a little pale and did not reply.

"You understand me, Kitty," I said. "There is nothing in the world that I care for but you. What have you to say to me?"

Then came back to her her little smile. "I think it would be very foolish for us to go away," she said.

It was about a quarter of an hour after this when Kitty proposed that we should go out to the front of the house. It would look queer if any of the servants should come by and see us sitting together like that. I had forgotten that there were other people in the world; but I went with her.

We were standing on the front porch close to each other, and I think we were holding each other's hands, when Mrs. Carson came back. As she approached she looked at us inquiringly, plainly wishing to know why we were standing side by side before her door as if we had some special object in so doing.

"Well?" said she, as she came up the steps. Of course it was right that I should speak, and, in as few words as possible, I told her what Kitty and I had been saying to each other. I never saw Kitty's mother look so cheerful and so handsome as when she came forward and kissed her daughter and shook hands with me. She seemed so perfectly satisfied that it amazed me. After a little Kitty left us, and then Mrs. Carson asked me to sit by her on a rustic bench.

"Now," said she, "this will straighten out things in the very best way. When you are married, you and Kitty can live in the back building—for, of course, your house will now be the same thing as a back building—and you can have the second floor. We won't have any separate tables, because it will be a great deal nicer for you and Kitty to live with me, and it will simply be your paying board for two persons instead of one; and you know you can manage your vineyard just as well

from the bottom of the hill as from the top.
The lower rooms of what used to be your house
can be made very pleasant and comfortable
for all of us. I have been thinking about the
room on the right that you had planned for
a parlor, and it will make a lovely sitting-room
for us, which is a thing we have never had,
and the room on the other side is just what
will suit beautifully for a guest-chamber. The
two houses together, with the roof of my back
porch properly joined to the front of your
house, will make a beautiful and spacious
dwelling. It was fortunate, too, that you
painted your house a light yellow; I have
often looked at the two together, and thought
what a good thing it was that one was not one
color and the other another. And as to the
pump, it will be very easy now to put a pipe
from what used to be your back porch to our
kitchen, so that we can get water without being obliged to carry it. Between us we can
make all sorts of improvements, and some
time I will tell you of a good many that I
have thought of.

"What used to be your house," she continued, " can be jackscrewed up a little bit
and a good foundation put under it; I have

inquired about that. Of course it would not have been proper to let you know that I was satisfied with the state of things, but I was satisfied, and there is no use of denying it. As soon as I got over my first scare, after that house came down the hill, and had seen how everything might be arranged to suit all parties, I said to myself: ' What the Lord has joined together, let not man put asunder,' and so, according to my belief, the strongest kind of jackscrews could not put these two houses asunder, any more than they could put you and Kitty asunder, now that you have agreed to take each other for each other's own."

Jack Brandiger came to call that evening, and when he had heard what had happened he whistled a good deal. "You are a funny kind of a fellow," said he. "You go courting like a snail, with your house on your back!"

I think my friend was a little discomfited. "Don't be discouraged, Jack," said I. "You will get a good wife some of these days; that is, if you don't try to slide uphill to find her!"